# KRISTY AND THE
# SECRET OF SUSAN

## Other books by
## Ann M. Martin

*Rachel Parker, Kindergarten Show-off*
*Eleven Kids, One Summer*
*Ma and Pa Dracula*
*Yours Turly, Shirley*
*Ten Kids, No Pets*
*Slam Book*
*Just a Summer Romance*
*Missing Since Monday*
*With You and Without You*
*Me and Katie (the Pest)*
*Stage Fright*
*Inside Out*
*Bummer Summer*

BABY-SITTERS LITTLE SISTER series
THE BABY-SITTERS CLUB mysteries
THE BABY-SITTERS CLUB series

# THE BABY-SITTERS CLUB

## KRISTY AND THE
## SECRET OF SUSAN

# Ann M. Martin

AN
**APPLE**
PAPERBACK

SCHOLASTIC INC.
New York Toronto London Auckland Sydney

*For David Holmes*

Cover art by Hodges Soileau

No part of this publication may be reproduced in whole or in part, or stored in a retrieval system, or transmitted in any form or by any means, electronic, mechanical, photocopying, recording, or otherwise, without written permission of the publisher. For information regarding permission, write to Scholastic Inc., 555 Broadway, New York, NY 10012.

ISBN 0-590-73189-0

12 11 10 9 8 7 6                          4                          0 1/0

Printed in the U.S.A.                                                  40

# CHAPTER 1

"Kristy! Emily did it again!"

"What? What did she do?" I asked.

My brother David Michael was yelling to me from the den, where he and our little sister Emily were playing. I was in the kitchen fixing an after-school snack for David Michael and a bottle of milk for Emily.

"She got the remote control," David Michael yelled. "She's changing channels on the TV. And I want to watch *Gorilla Man*."

"Well, put the remote control up high where she can't reach it," I called back.

I was screwing the lid on Emily's bottle when I heard a shriek. It was Emily. When you're around kids as much as I am, you get to know whose shriek is whose.

"Now what's wrong?" I asked as I entered the den, carrying the bottle and David Michael's snack. Emily was jumping up and

1

down and crying. Well, she wasn't exactly jumping, since she can't get her feet off the ground yet. She was just doing fast knee-bends. And her face was as red as a tomato.

"Wah-ah-ah-ah-ah-ah," she wailed in frustration.

David Michael looked flustered. "I did exactly what you told me to do," he said. "I put the remote control up there," (he pointed to a shelf) "and Emily began crying."

"Well, don't worry," I said. "You didn't do anything wrong. Look, here's your snack." I handed him half a sandwich. "You eat that and I'll calm Emily down."

What a wild family I have. I love baby-sitting for my little brothers and sisters (there are four of them all together — I'll explain that in a minute), but sometimes things can get touchy.

David Michael sat at one end of the couch in the den, eating his sandwich, watching *Gorilla Man*, and occasionally casting wounded glances in my direction.

Meanwhile, I tried to calm Emily down. I sat her on my lap in the armchair and explained that the remote control is for bigger people who know what all the buttons do. Then I said that it was polite to ask somebody if you could change channels before you actually *did* it. I purposely said that, instead of saying that what Emily had done was rude or wrong or bad. With children — or with anyone for that matter — it's much more helpful to tell them what *to* do instead of what *not* to do. Also, children are sensitive and I didn't want to hurt Emily's feelings.

All my talk was probably wasted, though. See, Emily is our adopted sister. She's two years old and she came to us from Vietnam. So first of all, she doesn't talk much, and second, she's just beginning to understand English.

I told you I have a wild family. Here are the people in it: Mom; my stepfather, Watson Brewer; my seventeen-year-old brother, Charlie; my fifteen-year-old brother, Sam; David Michael (he's seven); Emily; Karen and Andrew, who are Watson's kids from his first marriage (Karen is seven and Andrew is almost five); and Nannie. Nannie is Mom's mother, my grandmother. She moved in with us after we adopted Emily. Nannie's husband had died years earlier, Nannie was tired of living alone, and we needed someone to help care for Emily, since both Mom and Watson work.

As you can imagine, we need a pretty big

house for all these people. Luckily, Watson just happens to be a millionaire. Honest. He really is. So after he and Mom got married, my family moved across town to live in his mansion. The house is so big that everyone has his or her own room, even Karen and Andrew, who only live with us every other weekend.

What happened to my real father? He walked out on Mom and my brothers and me not long after David Michael was born, and we hardly ever hear from him. He usually forgets our birthdays. Sometimes he even forgets to send us Christmas presents or cards. All I know about him now is that he's living in California somewhere. Or at least he was the last time he bothered to call. We live in Stoneybrook, Connecticut, so my father is about as far away from us as he can get without leaving the continental United States.

Oh! I almost forgot! My name is Kristy Thomas and I'm thirteen and in eighth grade. And there are two other members of the Brewer/Thomas household — Shannon, who is David Michael's puppy (she's a Bernese mountain dog), and Boo-Boo, Watson's cat. Nobody except Watson likes Boo-Boo very much. Boo-Boo is old and fat and cranky. If

4

you're not careful, he'll scratch or bite you. But for some reason, he likes Shannon.

On that particular afternoon, I was baby-sitting because everyone else was busy. Mom and Watson were at their jobs, Charlie and Sam were at after-school activities at Stoneybrook High School, and Nannie was at bowling practice. That is one of the things I just love about Nannie. She doesn't seem like a grandmother at all. Her hair is barely gray, she's got tons of energy and is always off bowling or visiting friends or something, and she drives this rattly old car, which she painted pink and named the Pink Clinker. Recently, she attached a fake tail to the back of her car so that it looks like a cat is stuck in the trunk. (Charlie and Sam are embarrassed to be seen riding in the Pink Clinker.)

When David Michael and Emily had calmed down and been playing happily for awhile, I checked my watch. It was almost five o'clock. Soon Nannie would come home, and then Charlie and Sam would arrive from school. Charlie bought a used car not long ago so he can drive himself and Sam to school every day. The two of them think they are pretty cool.

A little while later I heard Emily's bare feet running through the house, and her cries of,

"Nannie! Nannie!" ("Nannie" is an easy word to say.)

Sure enough, Nannie was back. The Pink Clinker was sitting in the driveway. Five minutes later, another car pulled in and Sam ran into the house.

"Hello!" he called. "I'm home! Kristy, Charlie's waiting to drive you to your club meeting."

"Okay! Good-bye, everyone!" I shouted. It was time for the changing of the guards. Nannie would begin fixing dinner, and Sam would watch Emily and David Michael.

I dashed out to Charlie's car. It is just as clunky as Nannie's. It isn't painted pink, but it's got a pair of sunglasses hanging from the rearview mirror and one of those yellow signs stuck on the back window. Charlie made the sign himself. It says "Baby-sitter on Board," since he drives me around so much and I am the president and founder of a business called The Baby-sitters Club (or the BSC). In fact, that was where he was driving me now — across Stoneybrook to my friend Claudia Kishi's house for a club meeting. Claud's bedroom is BSC headquarters.

When we reached the Kishis' house, Charlie pulled up in front, and I ran right inside and upstairs to Claud's room. The BSC members usually don't bother to ring the Kishis' bell. I feel especially comfortable barging into her house, since I lived across the street from her before my family moved to Watson's.

"Hi, everybody!" I said as I entered Claud's room.

"Everybody" was Dawn Schafer and Claudia. (Dawn is another club member.) The two of them were spying out the window.

"What's going on?" I asked. I joined them at the window.

"The new people are moving in across the street," replied Dawn.

"Oh, into Mary Anne's old house," I said. Another club member, Mary Anne Spier, who used to be my next-door neighbor, had moved recently. My old house had been bought by a really nice family, the Perkinses. Now someone had bought Mary Anne's house.

"Yeah, I noticed them when Charlie dropped me off," I continued. "Do they have any kids?"

"Do they ever!" exclaimed Claudia. "Four boys, as far as we can tell. The oldest one looks like he's about eleven or twelve. He's kind of cute."

"But that's not the best part," said Dawn,

sounding terribly excited. "Guess what —
they're Aussies!"

"They're *what*?" I cried.

"Aussies. From Australia."

"You mean Crocodile Dundee and all that
stuff?" I asked, fascinated. Then I added, "Is
'Aussies' a nice word?"

"I don't know," replied Dawn. "But you
should hear their accents. They're wonderful."

"Hear their accents?" I repeated. "How long
have you guys been spying?"

"About fifteen minutes," Claudia admitted
guiltily. "We couldn't help it. Dawn came over
early, and the boys were out front talking
about crickets or something, and she heard
their accents, and then we started watching
their furniture come off the van, and — "

"I wonder how they got their furniture here
from halfway around the world," interrupted
Dawn, looking puzzled. "Did they ship it on a
boat and then transfer it to the van, or did — "

Now it was my turn to interrupt. I'd been
watching the Aussies, too, but my attention
had been distracted. Walking down the street
in our direction was a tired-looking woman
leading a little girl by the hand. The girl looked
like she was seven, maybe eight years old.

And when I say the woman was leading the girl, I mean she was *leading* her. The girl was lagging several paces behind and looked as if she didn't want to be out walking *or* holding anyone's hand. Plus, she looked sort of . . . odd. She moved strangely, holding her head to one side and looking ahead out of the corners of her eyes. And she took quick, short steps in a stiff, uncomfortable way, and flapped her free hand in front of her face.

"Hey," I said to my friends. "Who're they?" I pointed down the street. "Are they new here, too?"

"No," replied Claudia, looking slightly surprised. "Don't you remember the Felders? They live around the corner."

I thought for a minute. I did vaguely remember a Mr. and Mrs. Felder, but no little girl. "Is that their daughter?" I asked.

"Yeah," said Claud. "Susan. She's been living at a special school, but I guess she's home now. That's probably why you don't remember her. Because she's been away. The Felders don't have any other kids."

"Oh," I said, frowning. I watched Susan and her mother turn a corner. Then I went back to watching the Aussies. So did Dawn and Claud. We watched until the other club members began to show up. When everyone had arrived, it was time to start another meeting of the BSC. I surveyed the club members. Everyone was ready.

# CHAPTER 2

I feel very lucky. Not only do I have an interesting family, but I've got the most terrific group of friends you can imagine. There are seven people in the BSC — Mary Anne Spier, Claudia Kishi, Stacey McGill, Dawn Schafer, Jessi Ramsey, Mallory Pike, and me. (Two other people who are sort of club members, but who don't usually come to meetings, are Logan Bruno and Shannon Kilbourne. I'll tell you more about them later.)

My best friend in the club is Mary Anne Spier. For the longest time, Mary Anne and I lived next door to each other and across the street from Claudia. In fact, since we're all thirteen, we were born around the same time and grew up together. Then I moved to a different neighborhood and then Mary Anne moved, but that barely changed our friendship.

11

Anyway, considering we are best friends, Mary Anne and I sure are different. For one thing, I hate to admit it, but I have sort of a big mouth. My mouth has gotten me into trouble more times than I care to mention. I never *mean* to be rude or insulting, but things pop into my head and I can't help saying them. That's just the way I am. Also, I'm a tomboy and I love sports, especially softball. I even coach a softball team of little kids here in Stoneybrook. The team is called Kristy's Krushers.

I'm only just beginning to be interested in boys, and I don't care too much about clothes. I dress for comfort, which means that I almost always wear jeans, a turtleneck shirt, and running shoes. If it's cold out, I add a sweater, usually a pullover. If I feel like it, I wear a baseball cap. My favorite one has a collie on it. (Before David Michael got Shannon, we had a collie named Louie, who was the best dog in the world. But Louie got very sick and we had to have him put to sleep.) Well, I'm off the subject. What I'm trying to get at is how different Mary Anne and I are, so let me tell you about Mary Anne.

Mary Anne Spier is as quiet and shy as I am outspoken and outgoing. She's sensitive, romantic, and a good listener. Often, if one of us has a problem, we take it to Mary Anne. She may not have an answer, but she listens so sympathetically that you feel better just because you've told her about whatever is wrong. Mary Anne is also a big crier. She cries at movies (sad ones and happy ones), when her feelings are hurt, when someone else's feelings are hurt, or when people are angry. We've all gotten used to this.

Despite the fact that she's shy, Mary Anne is the first one of us to have a steady boyfriend. He's Logan Bruno, one of our associate club members! Logan and Mary Anne were made for each other. Logan has a great sense of humor, and he understands Mary Anne and her feelings and moods. He wouldn't mind, for instance, if they went to a school dance and Mary Anne suddenly felt too shy to dance.

Mary Anne's family *used* to be the exact opposite of mine, but now it's similar. See, Mrs. Spier died years ago, when Mary Anne was really little. So Mary Anne grew up with just a dad — no mom or brothers or sisters. And her dad was very strict with her, I think because he was trying to prove that he could be both mother and father to his daughter. He made up all these rules about how Mary Anne

13

had to dress and wear her hair, when she could use the phone, where she could go with friends, and how she could spend her money. Then, almost a year ago, Mary Anne began standing up for herself. She showed her father that she wasn't a little girl anymore, but a responsible young adult, so he loosened up. Not long after that, Mary Anne began to dress more stylishly and she started going out with Logan.

Then the unexpected happened. Mr. Spier met Dawn Schafer's mother and recently they *got married!* No kidding. It turned out that he had known Mrs. Schafer in high school (when she was Sharon Porter) and they'd been in love. But Mrs. Schafer had moved to California, married Dawn's father, had Dawn and her brother, Jeff, and then decided to get divorced. After that happened, she moved her kids back here to Stoneybrook, where she'd grown up, and the rest is history. Mary Anne and her father now live in the Schafers' house (it's bigger than theirs was) and Mary Anne has a stepmother, a stepbrother, and a stepsister — Dawn. Mary Anne, by the way, just happens to be Dawn's best friend!

Two things that are the same about Mary Anne and me are that we like animals (Mary

Anne has a kitten named Tigger), and we look sort of alike. We're both short (I'm actually the shortest girl in my whole class), and we both have brown eyes and brown hair. Mary Anne is more apt to *do* things with her hair, though — to French braid it, or to wear headbands or hair ribbons or bows. I don't think I'm as pretty as Mary Anne is.

Maybe I better tell you about Dawn next, since you've already heard a little about her family. I'll start by saying that Dawn is dropdead gorgeous — but I don't think she knows it or would care much about it if she did know. Dawn has the longest, palest blonde hair I've ever seen. It's the color of corn silk, and if it grows much longer, she'll be able to sit on it. (Well, maybe that's an exaggeration.) She has sparkly blue eyes, is tall and slender, has two holes pierced in each ear, and dresses in a style that my friends and I call California casual.

"Casual" is a pretty good way to describe Dawn herself. She's very laid-back. For the most part, she doesn't care what people think of her and just sort of goes her own way. (I'm hoping a little of that will rub off on Mary Anne.) Dawn does have chinks in her armor, though. Every now and then, something will cut deep enough so that Dawn feels hurt or anxious. But not often. She's easygoing, a caring stepsister to Mary Anne, and a good friend to the rest of us.

As I mentioned before, Dawn grew up in California. Moving to the East Coast was hard for her. Not only did she leave her father behind, but she misses the warm weather. Dawn is happiest when July and August come to Stoneybrook. Maybe because of California (or maybe not) Dawn is also a health-food nut. So's the rest of her family. They don't eat meat or junk food, and they love vegetables, fruit, and gross stuff like tofu.

Oops, I've gotten off the subject again. Anyway, Dawn, Jeff, and their mom moved to Stoneybrook — but Jeff, who's nine or ten, was never happy here, so he finally moved back to California to live with his father. I know Dawn was terribly hurt then. Her family was split in half and separated by three thousand miles. But she's happier now that she has another family. At first, everyone had some problems getting adjusted, but Mary Anne's organized, finicky father turned out to be a good husband for Dawn's disorganized, scatterbrained mother. And Dawn loves having a sister. She had always wanted one.

Guess what one of Dawn's favorite activities

is — reading ghost stories. And guess where she lives — in a centuries-old farmhouse with an actual *secret passage* in it. This is the truth, although it's hard to believe. The passage may even be haunted, but we're not sure.

Okay, on to Claudia. Claudia Kishi, the vice-president of the BSC, is as gorgeous as Dawn, even though the two of them don't look a thing alike. Claud is Japanese-American. Both of her parents are Japanese, but Claud was born here in Stoneybrook. She has very long, silky, jet-black hair; dark, almond-shaped eyes; and a creamy complexion. Like Dawn, she's got pierced ears, too, only she has one hole in one ear and two in the other. (By the way, Mary Anne and I do *not* have pierced ears and intend to keep them like that — intact.) Anyway, aside from being beautiful, Claudia is also an incredibly cool dresser and an incredibly talented artist. You should see her clothes. She's always wearing short flared skirts, or leggings, or ankle socks and flat shoes, whatever is *the* most cool fashion at the moment. I don't know how she knows what's cool. Maybe she reads magazines or something. Claudia is also especially good at accessorizing. Again, she just knows how to do it. And she spends a lot of her baby-sitting money on the accessories — belts, jewelry, and tons of stuff for her hair — ribbons, bows, funky clips, beads. She wears her hair a million different ways. I've never seen anyone who can come up with so many styles.

Claudia *makes* some of her own jewelry — ceramic earrings and pins, papier-mâché bracelets, that sort of thing. Claud can draw, paint, sculpt, make pottery, you name it. I'm glad she's good at art because she's terrible in school, although she's smart. For some reason, school is just hard for Claud, and she doesn't like it. She gets only average grades and she's the world's worst speller. Unfortunately, her sister, Janine, is a genius. She's so smart that even though she's a high-school student she gets to take courses at the local community college. For pleasure, Janine reads stuff like *Atomic Theory* or *The History of Law-making in America*. Claud reads Nancy Drew books, but her parents don't approve of them, so she has to hide them in her room.

Books aren't the only thing she hides. Claudia is also a junk-food addict, something else her parents disapprove of. So there are bags of chips and candy, and packages of Twinkies and Oreos hidden in her room, too. Opening a drawer in Claud's room, or going after something that's rolled under her bed, can be a surprising experience.

Claudia's best friend is Stacey McGill, and the two of them are alike in a lot of ways. Stacey is also very sophisticated, quite pretty, and *extremely* cool. She's as funky a dresser as Claud — short, tight pants, push-down socks, the whole bit. Every now and then she gets her hair permed, and, of course, she's got pierced ears.

Claudia and Stacey are boy-crazy.

However, Stacey's home life is different from Claud's. And if you think my family, or Mary Anne and Dawn's family, is interesting, you should hear about Stacey's. Stacey, whose full name is Anastasia Elizabeth McGill, was born and raised in *New York City*. No wonder she's so sophisticated. Then, just before she began seventh grade, the company her father works for transferred him to their office in Stamford, Connecticut, so the McGills found a house in Stoneybrook and moved here. They'd only been here a year when the company moved Mr. McGill *back* to New York. None of us could believe it, but the McGills had to go. *Then*, they'd been in NYC again for *less* than a year when Stacey's parents got separated and then divorced. Mr. McGill stayed in NYC with his job, but Mrs. McGill wanted to come back to Connecticut. Poor Stacey had to choose where to live. She decided on Stoneybrook and us and the BSC, thank goodness, but she visits her dad in New York a lot.

Another thing about Stacey is that she has diabetes. That's a disease in which her pancreas doesn't make enough of something called insulin, so her blood sugar level gets out of control. Stacey has to give herself injections (ew, ew, ew) of insulin every day, and also stay on a *strict* no-sugar diet. Otherwise, she could get really sick. She could even go into a coma. It must be hard for her to have to turn down Claud's junk food all the time.

Guess what. When Stacey and her mom moved back to Connecticut, they couldn't move into their old house. That was because Jessi had moved into it! Jessi Ramsey and Mallory Pike are the two younger members of the BSC. They're best friends, eleven years old, and in sixth grade at Stoneybrook Middle School. The rest of us are in eighth grade.

Like Stacey and Claudia, Jessi and Mal are alike in many ways and different in many ways. They're each the oldest kid in their families, and they think their parents treat them like babies. I guess it *is* hard being eleven. I remember wanting so badly to be more grown-up when I was their age, but Mom didn't start really letting me grow up until I was twelve. Anyway, Jessi and Mal have campaigned hard to be allowed to do more things, and their parents *did* let them get their ears pierced (just one hole in each ear). However, Mal then had to have braces put on her teeth, and she wears glasses and isn't allowed to get contacts, so she's not feeling particularly pretty these days, even with her pierced ears.

Jessi and Mal both love to read, especially horse stories by Marguerite Henry. Beyond that, they're quite different. Jessi's passion is ballet, and boy, is she good. She takes special classes at a dance school in Stamford, where she had to audition just to get in, and she has danced lead roles in productions before hundreds of people. Mal's passions are writing and drawing, and she thinks she'd like to be an author and illustrator of children's books when she grows up. Jessi comes from an average-sized family — her parents, an eight-year-old sister named Becca, and a baby brother nicknamed Squirt — while Mal comes from a *huge* family. Her parents have eight children! Mal has four brothers (three of them are identical triplets) and three sisters. Another difference is that Jessi is black and Mal is white. This doesn't matter to them, or to any of us in the BSC, but Jessi's skin color bothered a lot of people in Stoneybrook, I'm ashamed to say. The Ramseys' neighbors gave them a really hard time at first, although they've calmed down now. They've found that there's not a thing to dislike about the Ramseys.

Oh, I forgot one other similarity between Jessi and Mal. Each of their families has a pet hamster!

Okay. So now you know the members of the Baby-sitters Club. A meeting was about to begin. I put on my visor, sat down in Claud's director's chair, stuck a pencil over my ear, and called the meeting to order.

## CHAPTER 3

$A$s president of the BSC, I feel it is my duty to run our meetings professionally and in a businesslike manner. We have done that since the club first started. How did the BSC begin? Well, it began because of David Michael, really. See, back at the start of seventh grade, when Mom and Watson weren't even talking about getting married, my mother and brothers and I still lived on Bradford Court, next door to Mary Anne and across from Claudia. In those days, Sam and Charlie and I were responsible for taking care of David Michael after school until Mom came home from work. We took turns. But, of course, an evening came when we realized that none of us was free to baby-sit for him the next day, so Mom had to find another sitter on short notice. It wasn't easy. I remember we were eating pizza for dinner that night, and I sat there with my

23

slice, watching Mom make call after call. Nobody was available — and Mom was wasting a lot of time on the phone.

That was when I got my greatest idea ever. Wouldn't it be neat if Mom could make just *one* call and reach a whole lot of sitters at once? As soon as I could, I told Mary Anne and Claudia that I'd thought of a business we could start. We could form a baby-sitting club and meet several times a week. Then people could call us during those times and reach three responsible, reliable sitters. (We were already baby-sitting a lot in our neighborhood.) With several people at the other end of the phone, the caller was bound to find an available sitter.

My friends thought this was a great idea, too, but they also thought three people weren't enough. So we asked Stacey, who was just getting to know Claudia then, if she wanted to join, and she said yes! A few months later, when Dawn moved to Stoneybrook, our club was doing so much business that we asked her to join, too. Then when Stacey had to move back to New York, we couldn't do without her, so both Jessi and Mal joined the club. And *then* Stacey returned to Stoneybrook. We welcomed her back into the club, of course. As an original member and a good friend, we'd never have turned her away. Plus, we needed her. I think, though, that with seven members plus our two associate members, Logan and Shannon, the BSC is finally big enough.

Here's how our club operates. The seven members meet three afternoons a week — Mondays, Wednesdays, and Fridays from five-thirty until six. Our clients call us at those times to line up baby-sitters. They know they'll get one. It's unlikely that every single one of us *plus* Logan and Shannon would be busy.

How do clients hear about our club and know when and how to reach us? Because we advertise. Before we even started the club, we distributed dozens of fliers in our neighborhood, and we even placed an ad in the Stoneybrook newspaper. Now we send out fliers occasionally, but we don't really need to. News of our club spreads by word of mouth, plus we have as much business as we can handle.

Every member of the club (except for Logan and Shannon) is an officer.

I am the president. This is mostly because I thought up the club in the first place, and also because I'm good at solving problems, running the club, and thinking up new ideas.

For instance, I decided that we should keep a club notebook. It's sort of like a diary. In it, my friends and I write up every single job we go on. Then, once a week, we read the recent diary entries to see what went on when our friends were baby-sitting. Nobody (except Mallory) really likes to write in the diary, but we all agree that reading it is helpful. We find out what's going on with the kids we take care of, and how our friends solve sitting problems.

Another of my ideas was that we should each make a Kid-Kit. Kid-Kits are boxes that we decorated with paint and felt and sequins and things, and filled with our old games, books, and toys, plus some new items such as sticker books, crayons, and drawing paper. Children just love playing with the stuff in the Kid-Kits. For some reason, other people's toys are always more interesting than theirs. And happy baby-sitting charges mean happy parents who are apt to call the BSC again with more jobs!

Claudia is the vice-president of the club. She's the only one of us with a phone in her room and her own phone number. This is an ideal situation. If we had to use some adult's phone, we'd feel that we were tying it up. Plus, nonbaby-sitting calls would come in and interrupt our meetings. We think it's only fair that Claud be the VP, since we invade her room three times a week, use her phone, and eat her junk food.

Mary Anne is the club secretary. She has the biggest, most complicated job of any of us. As secretary, it's up to Mary Anne to keep our club record book (don't confuse that with the notebook) up to date. In the record book is all the important club information — names and addresses of our clients, the money we earn (recording that is really Stacey's job), and most important of all, the appointment pages. On those pages, Mary Anne schedules every single sitting job we go on. In order to do that, she has to know all of our schedules — when Mal has orthodontist appointments or I've got a Krushers game or Jessi has ballet classes. So far, Mary Anne hasn't made a single mistake. She's amazing.

Stacey is our treasurer. Since she loves money and is a math whiz, this is the perfect job for her. Every Monday, Stacey collects our club dues and adds it to the treasury (which is a manila envelope). Then she doles out money whenever it's needed, usually for four things — new items for the Kid-Kits, to help pay for Claud's phone bill, to pay Charlie to drive me to and from meetings, since I live so far from BSC headquarters now, and to buy supplies for occasional club treats such as pizza parties or sleepovers. Stacey loves collecting the money and hates parting with it.

Dawn is our alternate officer. This means that if any club member has to miss a meeting, Dawn can take over her job for her. She's like a substitute teacher: she has to know what everyone does. When Stacey moved back to New York for that short time, Dawn became the treasurer. But she gladly gave up the job when Stacey returned. She's not nearly as good at math as Stacey is.

Jessi and Mal are junior officers. They don't actually have jobs. "Junior officer" means that they're only allowed to baby-sit after school or on weekends. They can't sit at night unless they're sitting for their own families. They are a huge help to us older members, though. Since they take on after-school jobs, they free the rest of us up for evening jobs.

Then there are our associate members, Logan and Shannon. As I mentioned before, they don't come to meetings. They're just reliable sitters we can call on if a job is offered to the BSC that none of the rest of us can take. Believe it or not, this happens from time to time. (In case you're wondering, Shannon Kilbourne is a friend of mine. She lives across the street from me in my new neighborhood. And she's the only one of us club members who doesn't go to Stoneybrook Middle School. Instead, she goes to a private school.)

And that's how we operate our club.

"Order! Order, please!" I called.

My friends stopped talking. Claudia turned away from the window, which she'd been about to peer out of again.

Everyone was sitting in her usual place. I was in the director's chair, as I mentioned; Jessi and Mal were sitting on the floor, leaning against Claud's bed; Claud, Dawn, and Mary Anne were sitting in a row on the bed, leaning against the wall; and Stacey was sitting backwards in Claud's desk chair, her arms draped over the top rung. (Sometimes Stacey sits on the bed and Dawn sits in the desk chair.)

Since it was Wednesday and not Monday, Stacey didn't have to collect dues. So I asked, "Any club business?"

Six heads shook from side to side.

We waited for the phone to ring.

We'd lined up three jobs when, at 5:50, the phone rang for a fourth time. I answered it. "Hello, Baby-sitters Club."

"Hello," said an unfamiliar voice. "My name is Mrs. Felder."

"Oh, Mrs. Felder," I said. "This is Kristy Thomas. I used to live around the corner from you." (Even though I didn't really remember Mrs. Felder, maybe she remembered me.)

"Hi, Kristy," she replied warmly. "I'm calling because I heard how wonderful your baby-sitting business is. And I've got a daughter, Susan. She's handicapped — autistic actually — and she's been living at a special school, but now she's home for a month, waiting to be transferred to a new school. I don't work, but I'd like a break from Susan three afternoons a week if possible. Just for a couple of hours each time so I can get out and go to the store, that sort of thing. Do you think any of you would be able to take on a job like that?"

"I'll have to check," I told Mrs. Felder. "I'll call you right back."

I hung up the phone and explained the job to my friends.

"Gosh," said Mary Anne, "that's going to be tough, scheduling-wise."

"What did you say is wrong with Susan?" asked Jessi.

"She's autistic. I think that's the word Mrs. Felder used. But I'm not sure what it means."

"Retarded?" suggested Claudia.

I shrugged.

"Well, anyway," said Mary Anne, "Kristy, it looks like you're the only one of us who could sit for Susan three times a week for a month. You don't have any lessons or anything, and if you went to the Felders on Mondays, Wednesdays, and Fridays, you wouldn't even have to cancel a Krushers practice or the sitting jobs you've already got lined up."

"Hmm," I said. "Charlie has to drive me over here for meetings on those days anyway. Maybe he could do it right after school instead of at five-thirty. Then he could pick me up at the regular time. Let me call Charlie."

So I did, and he said he could work that into his schedule. Then he added, "For a small additional fee, of course," but it turned out he was only kidding.

"Well, this is good news," I told my friends. "I can't believe we scheduled this so easily. Mary Anne, pencil me in for Susan for the next month, and I'll call Mrs. Felder back."

I dialed the Felders' number. "Hi," I said. "This is Kristy Thomas again, president of the Baby-sitters Club. I'm happy to tell you that I will be Susan's sitter for the next month. We worked out all the details."

Mrs. Felder didn't sound as happy as I'd expected. In fact, all she said was, "That's fine. But I think you better meet Susan before you make a final decision about the job, okay?"

"Okay," I replied uncertainly.

We decided that I would go to the Felders' on Friday before the next BSC meeting. What kind of child was Susan? I wondered. Why did Mrs. Felder think I might not want to sit for her? I was dying of curiosity.

# CHAPTER 4

Not far from Susan Felder lives a family, the Braddocks, with a deaf boy named Matt. Jessi once had a long-term sitting job for Matt and his sister, Haley — just like the one I was about to begin (maybe) with Susan. I remember Jessi saying how nervous she was the first time she rang the Braddocks' doorbell. What would Matt be like? she'd wondered. She knew he communicated using sign language. Would Jessi be able to learn enough sign language to talk with him? Would he be difficult to sit for? How would he react to a stranger?

Now I knew how Jessi had felt. Charlie had just dropped me off at the Felders', calling out the car window that he would pick me up after the BSC meeting. He had driven away, and now I was standing on the Felders' front stoop, my finger poised to ring the bell.

What would Susan be like? All I knew of

33

her was what I had seen when she'd been out walking — a reluctant-looking little girl who made strange gestures and movements. And I knew she'd gone to a "special" school. But what kind of school exactly? Mrs. Felder had hinted that I might not want the job once I met Susan.

I had looked up "autistic" in the dictionary. I couldn't find the word, but I had found "autism." The definition said something about childhood schizophrenia, acting out, and withdrawal. That was no help. Then I looked up "schizophrenia," but I was more confused than ever. The definition mentioned "withdrawing from reality." For heaven's sake, I am always withdrawing from reality — every time I daydream. And my stepsister, Karen, believes in ghosts and witches, but there's nothing wrong with her. I would have to wait and see what Mrs. Felder said.

I rang the doorbell.

I could hear a piano playing. It stopped when the bell rang. A few moments later, Mrs. Felder was at the door.

"Kristy?" she said.

"Yes," I replied. "Hi, Mrs. Felder."

"Goodness, you've grown," was her reply, as she held the door open for me.

"Really?" I said. "Thanks. I'm still the shortest person in my class, though."

"I guess I haven't seen you in awhile. I knew your family better when David Michael was little. Your mom and I tried to set up play dates for him and Susan, but Susan was already . . . different. Even then. She's eight now. How old is David Michael? He must be almost eight."

"Yup. He's seven and a half," I replied.

Mrs. Felder nodded. She had led me into the living room, which was bright and sunny. A grand piano filled almost a quarter of the room. And walking restlessly back and forth in front of it was the little girl I had seen out Claudia's window.

Susan.

She was wringing her hands in front of her and making clicking noises with her mouth. She didn't look at either her mother or me.

"Susan?" said Mrs. Felder. "Susan? . . . Susan!"

Susan continued walking and flapping and clicking.

"*Susan!*" said Mrs. Felder more loudly. "Come here, please."

Like a sleeper waking from a dream, Susan turned and walked toward us. Her eyes were fixed on some point above our heads.

"Susan, this is Kristy," said Mrs. Felder.

"Hi," I said, getting my first close-up look at Susan Felder. And I saw that she was beautiful. Her eyes were wide and deep brown, and her hair, which was almost as dark as Claudia's, fell in soft curls to her shoulders. She could be a model, I thought.

Since Susan hadn't answered me, I said, "Hi," again.

Susan, still staring into outer space, wrung her hands a few times. Then she turned and flapped her way back to the piano.

I looked at Susan's mother. My eyes must have been question marks.

"She doesn't speak," said Mrs. Felder. "She could, but she doesn't. She can sing, though. Come on. Let's sit on the couch and I'll tell you about Susan."

I almost said, "In front of her?" but I realized that Susan probably would not be listening.

Mrs. Felder and I sat down, and I said, "I looked up autism in the dictionary, but I didn't understand the definition."

Mrs. Felder smiled. "I'm not surprised. There's a lot more to autism than anyone could fit into a dictionary definition. The best way I can describe it to you — and the symptoms vary from person to person — is that Susan is in her own world, and she doesn't seem to want to leave it. She doesn't communicate with anyone, she exhibits the strange behavior you see now — wringing her hands, clicking her tongue — and she rarely makes eye contact with anyone. Also, she doesn't much like to be touched or hugged, even by her father and me.''

"What caused it?'' I whispered, awed.

Mrs. Felder shook her head. "No one is certain. What we do know is that autistic symptoms always show up by the time a child is three — usually earlier, that most autistic people are boys, and that the syndrome is rare.''

"Will Susan get better?'' I asked.

"Maybe. Some educators and doctors believe that if an autistic child starts acquiring meaningful language by the time he's five, he can become much better. That hasn't happened for Susan. She can sing, but she has no *meaningful* language. Even those children who do acquire some speech will probably never be what most people consider 'normal.' They might be able to live in a group home, work part-time at a job or in a sheltered workshop — but that's about it.''

I just nodded. I understood what Mrs. Felder *wasn't* saying: Susan's future looked bleak.

Just when I was beginning to feel terribly sad, though, Mrs. Felder spoke again. "We're somewhat encouraged, her father and I," she said almost proudly, "because Susan is autistic but she's also a savant. That means she has some very specialized talents."

"Really?" I asked, intrigued.

"Yes. Although Susan is untestable, her IQ is thought to be below fifty, which is extremely retarded. But you should hear her play the piano." Mrs. Felder smiled. And I began to feel hopeful instead of sad. "She's really remarkable," Mrs. Felder went on. "She astonishes everyone — her teachers, her doctors, even *music* teachers. She can usually play any new piece of music after hearing it only once. Just like that — she's got the whole thing memorized *and* she can play it. She can play long, long scores, and any type of music — classical, ballads, show tunes, you name it. She can even play something she's only heard played on another instrument, such as the violin."

"How does she do that?" I asked. I was amazed.

"Nobody is sure. I do play the piano myself, and when Susan was little I used to entertain her by sitting her next to me and teaching her simple songs. But then she just took off. Believe me, I can't do what Susan does.

"Oh," Mrs. Felder continued, "if a piece of music has words to it — in any language — Susan can also memorize the song after hearing it once, and sing it while she plays. She has perfect pitch. We don't think the words mean anything to her, they're just more things to memorize, but singing and playing the piano seem to make her happy. She'd play all day if we let her. In fact, her musical abilities are the reason she's between schools right now. We're in the process of transferring her to a school with a strong music program. It's about an hour outside of Stoneybrook. The teachers and Mr. Felder and I are hoping that, through music, Susan can acquire some meaningful language as well as some social skills. We feel this is the best way to reach her. Of course, we want her to study music for its own sake, too.

"One more thing," Mrs. Felder went on. "One other peculiar talent. Susan seems to have a calendar in her head. Although no one has ever explained days, weeks, months, or years to her, she can tell you the day of the week that any date fell on, as long as you don't go more than sixty years into the past or more than about twenty years into the future. She found a perpetual calendar once and seems to have memorized it."

"You're kidding!" I exclaimed.

"Nope," said Mrs. Felder, looking proud again, but mystified, too. "I'll show you. Think of a date that's important to you."

"Okay," I said. "Um . . . the date Emily, my adopted sister, was born."

"Do you know the day of the week that happened?"

"Yes."

"All right. Tell me just the date."

I told her. Mrs. Felder called Susan over and told *her*.

"Monday," said Susan in a monotone voice without hesitating. Then she flapped her hands and ran back to the piano.

"That's right!" I cried. "It *was* a Monday!"

"Susan is correct about ninety-five percent of the time." Mrs. Felder paused. "But if you ask her how she is, what she wants for dinner, if she has to use the bathroom . . . nothing. No response. She never initiates conversations, either. She just does not communicate.

She can be very trying at times, too. Stubborn. Especially if you want her to stop playing the piano. But she's never violent. . . . Do — do you still want the job?"

"Oh, yes!" I said. I guess you can tell by now that I was thoroughly fascinated with Susan. I'd never met anyone like her. I'd never even *heard* of anyone like her. I was also feeling just the teeniest bit angry, though. Susan was very special. That was obvious. But everyone treated her like some kind of outcast. Her parents were taking her out of one away-from-home school and putting her in another. Why couldn't they keep her with them? There are schools for handicapped kids around here. *Day* schools like the one Matt Braddock goes to in Stamford. There are also classes for handicapped kids in the public schools. And why didn't her parents try to help Susan make friends? She couldn't talk, but neither could Matt, and he had plenty of friends. The kids in his neighborhood learned some sign language so they could play with him.

I decided that I would not only take on the job with Susan, but that I would use the month I had with her to show the Felders that she could live and learn and make friends *at home*. She did not have to be an outcast.

"That's wonderful," Mrs. Felder said. "I'm delighted to find someone who will watch Susan for me. It takes a dedicated, patient person. So — Mondays, Wednesdays, and Fridays from three-thirty to five-thirty, right?"

"Right," I agreed.

"That will be a perfect break for me. And don't worry. Susan won't be upset when I leave. She never is. She has no connection to me or to anyone."

We'll see about that, I thought. But I just smiled and said, "Okay. That sounds easy."

"Would you like to take Susan outside for awhile?" asked Mrs. Felder. "It's only five o'clock. I know your meeting doesn't start for half an hour. You can have a dry run with Susan while I'm at home."

"Sure," I replied.

"Okay, Susan, come here," said Mrs. Felder, standing up. "Let's put your sweater on. . . . Susan? *Susan!*"

Was it always difficult to attract Susan's attention? I wondered about that as I watched Mrs. Felder button Susan into a sweater. (I guessed that Susan couldn't do that herself.)

When Susan was ready, I took her hand and started to lead her to the back door. She pulled away a little, but then she allowed me to take her into her yard. Mrs. Felder was right. Susan didn't so much as glance at her mother. She just followed me. Could she tell her mother and me apart?

I looked around Susan's backyard and saw a swing set, a sandbox, and a tricycle. The toys seemed a little babyish for an eight-year-old, but at least they would be something for Susan and me to play with.

"Come on, Susan. I'll give you a ride on the swing," I said, letting go of her hand.

But Susan had other ideas. As soon as she was free of me, she began to gallop back and forth across her yard (which was fenced in), clicking her tongue and wringing her hands. I let her go to it, partly because I didn't want to push her into anything right away — and partly because something was going on in the Hobarts' backyard, which I could see clearly from the Felders'. I couldn't help watching for a few minutes.

The Hobarts were the Australian family. Claudia had learned their names. And the four boys were in their yard, facing a bunch of neighborhood kids who weren't looking too friendly.

"You want *fairy floss?*" exclaimed one familiar-looking kid, snickering.

"Yeah! It's rad," said one of the younger Hobarts. "Totally cool."

What was fairy floss? Candy?

Then a girl said, "If you guys are so cool, do some Crocodile Dundee stuff for us and prove it."

I turned away. I had to watch Susan. But I felt like a fighter. I would have to battle for Susan — because I knew she needed me to battle for her. And I might have to battle for the Hobarts if the other kids didn't stop teasing them.

Nobody can say I don't stand up for what I believe in. (I think I learned that from Dawn.)

# CHAPTER 5

Tuesday

Oh, help. I think I'm in... a crush.

Mallory, that is very exciting, but it doesn't belong in the club notebook.

I know, Jessi. Okay. I'll get down to business.

No, I will. I'll start. You calm down.

All right.

Well, today Mal and I sat for her brothers and sisters, and what a time we had. We took them to the Hobarts' so the Australian kids could see that not everyone is going to tease them about their accents and stuff.

45

Yeah. They've had a hard time in school as well as at home. Why are kids so cruel, Jessi?

*I don't know, even though lots of people have been mean to me.*

Well, maybe we can make a difference. Anyway, I think today's baby-sitting adventure was a start.

*I hope you're right, Mal.*

For some reason, even though Tuesday afternoon was a beautiful day, the Pike kids didn't know what to do with themselves. When Jessi arrived to sit with Mal, she found the ten-year-old triplets — Adam, Byron, and Jordan — nine-year-old Vanessa, eight-year-old Nicky, seven-year-old Margo, and five-year-old Claire draped all over the furniture in the Pikes' rec room, looking bored out of their minds.

Mal was standing over them saying, "I hope you guys are going to find things to do today."

"Me, too," said Mrs. Pike as she hurried out the back door. "Please behave, kids. I'll be back by six."

" 'Bye, Mom," said Mal as the door closed behind her mother.

"Do, do. What can I do? I've lost my sock and I've lost my shoe," said Vanessa, the poet.

"You have not," pointed out Claire.

"I *know*," replied Vanessa. "I was just making a poem."

"A stupid poem," said Adam.

"It was *not* stupid!" exclaimed Vanessa.

"Kindergarten baby, stick your head in gravy — " Nicky began.

"Enough, enough, enough!" cried Mal. "Look. The weather is lovely. Why don't you guys go outside? You could ride your bicycles — "

"Nah," said Jordan.

" — or go skateboarding — "

"Nah," said Nicky.

"You could stay inside," suggested Jessi. "There are plenty of things to do here, too. You could play a game — "

"Nah," said Vanessa.

" — or," (Jessi couldn't believe she was about to suggest this), "you could watch TV."

"There's nothing good on," said Margo.

Silence.

Finally Nicky said, "You know, a new family moved into Mary Anne's old house. The Ho-

47

barts. James Hobart is in my class at school. He's really weird. He talks funny — "

"He's from Australia," said Mal. "He has an accent, that's all."

"Australia?" spoke up Byron. "You mean like Crocodile Dundee?"

"Well, yes," agreed Jessi.

"Crocodile Dundee can do all kinds of neat things," said Jordan. "I hope the Hobarts are like Crocodile."

"They're Crocs!" cried Nicky gleefully. "That's what everyone in my class calls James and his brothers. The Crocs!" Nicky snickered.

"You guys," said Mallory warningly. "That is not very nice. Remember when the kids here used to call us the Spiders?"

"The Spiders?" repeated Jessi, perplexed.

"Yeah, because there are eight of us," explained Vanessa, looking troubled. "Like the eight legs on a spider. We hated that name."

"I've been called worse," said Jessi quietly. "You don't even want to *know* all the names people have called me — and just because of the color of my skin."

"What names?" asked Margo.

"Never mind," replied Jessi, sounding tired. "Nothing as cute as Spider, believe me."

The Pike kids stared at their hands, their shoes, the floor. None of them could look at Jessi.

"Name-calling isn't very nice at all," Claire finally said in a small voice.

"No. It isn't," agreed Mal. "It hurts people's feelings."

" 'Silly-billy-goo-goo' doesn't hurt people's feelings, though," said Claire. "I'm not being mean when I say 'silly-billy-goo-goo.' " (Claire just loves to call people that name.)

"No, you're just being a jerkhead — just being silly," Nicky corrected himself.

"How about going over to the Hobarts' to play with the boys?" suggested Mal. "I bet they'd like to know that not every kid around here is going to be mean to them. We could go as *friendly* neighbors."

The younger Pike kids glanced at each other. Jessi and Mal could tell they felt guilty about having called the Hobarts the "Crocs."

"Okay," said Byron. "Let's go."

"I think you'll have fun. Maybe you'll learn something about Australia. It's not *that* different from the United States, you know. The kids speak English and they do lots of the same things you do," said Mal.

"Like what?" asked Nicky, as Jessi and Mal led the kids out of the house and Mal locked the door behind them.

"Like ride bicycles," replied Mal, "and go skateboarding and take ballet lessons and collect stickers and listen to music. They even dress the way we do. Jeans and stuff."

"Oh!" said Vanessa, looking surprised.

"Just remember," added Jessi, "not to call them the Crocs. They won't like that."

"What about silly-billy-goo-goos?" asked Claire.

"Better not," replied Mal. "I don't think they'd understand."

Jessi, Mal, and Mal's brothers and sisters walked to the Hobarts' and found the boys playing in front of their house. The oldest one was whizzing along the sidewalk on a skateboard. His hair was red, and he wore glasses like Mal. The two middle boys were riding their bikes, and the youngest one was on the front lawn with a brand-new toy truck.

When the Pikes and Jessi stopped in the yard, the boy with the truck began to cry. His oldest brother ran over to him.

"It's okay, Johnny," he said. "Don't worry." He looked at Jessi and Mal.

"We come in peace," said Mal, smiling. "Have no fear."

The boy grinned back at her. "Don't I know you?" he asked.

"Well . . . I'm in sixth grade at Stoneybrook Middle School," Mal replied.

"Oh. So am I. I must have seen you at school."

Mal and the boy looked at each other for so long that finally Jessi said, "I'm Jessi Ramsey. I'm in your grade, too."

The boy shook himself, as if he'd been daydreaming. "Sorry," he said. "I'm Ben Hobart. Over there is James. He's eight."

"He's in my class at school," spoke up Nicky.

"And that's Mathew," Ben went on. "He's six. And this is Johnny. He's four. He's a little upset. Some of the kids around here have teased him. Well, *us*, really."

"I know," said Mal. "We're sorry." She wanted to say something else, but all she could think of was that Ben was gorgeous. *His* red hair was much nicer than hers (she thought), so were his glasses, and he did not have braces on his teeth.

"Well," said Mal.

"Well," said Jessi.

"Well," said Ben.

Jessi was about to figure out how to get the younger kids to play together, when she realized they'd already figured it out on their own. James and Mathew had abandoned their bikes, Johnny had abandoned his truck, and the kids were standing in the front yard in a tight group. Vanessa was saying, "We'll teach you guys how to play Statues. It's really fun."

"I'll, um, I'll just go help them," Jessi said to Mal and Ben.

They barely heard her. "Okay," Mal managed to reply. She and Ben wandered over to the Hobarts' front stoop and sat down.

If they sat any closer, Jessi thought, smiling to herself, Mal would be in Ben's lap!

Jessi supervised the game of Statues. She had to give the Pike kids credit. Not one "Croc" slipped out of anybody's mouth, and Claire didn't call a single person, not even one of her brothers and sisters, a silly-billy-goo-goo. Jessi wasn't *too* surprised, though. The Hobarts might not have sounded "American," but they certainly looked it. They were all wearing jeans (James's were ripped fashionably at the knees), both James and Mathew were wearing Swatch watches, and their shirts were oversized and baggy. Johnny was even wearing a little pair of Reeboks.

Just when Jessi was congratulating herself and Mal on getting the kids together so happily, five other kids from the neighborhood — three boys and two girls — rode by on their bikes, stopping at the Hobarts'.

"Uh-oh," said Johnny.

"Hey, baby!" yelled one of the boys to Mathew, "whadja eat this morning?"

"For brecky? Weetbix and toast with Vegemite."

The five kids burst into laughter. "Brecky! Weetbix!"

James pretended not to notice. He swaggered over to the kids. "Great bike," he commented, touching one. "Hey, are you a head banger?" he asked, eyeing the boy's punk hair.

"No," said the boy sarcastically. "I'm a . . . Croc."

"Funny as a funeral," muttered James.

He might have gone on, getting deeper and deeper into trouble, but he was rescued by Mal, Jessi, and Ben.

"Get on out of here, rev heads," said Ben. The kids were about to say something about "rev heads" when Ben, who is tall, stepped close to them. The kids hastily rode off.

But one called over his shoulder, "See you later . . . *Crocodiles!*"

Jessi and the younger Pike kids went home that afternoon feeling both triumphant and embarrassed.

But Mal barely felt a thing. Her mind was in outer space.

# CHAPTER 6

"Hello, Baby-sitters Club. How may we help you?"

I was at another BSC meeting. It had just begun and I had just taken the first call of the day.

"Oh, hi, Mrs. Prezzioso," I said. I rolled my eyes at my fellow club members. Jenny, the Prezziosos' only child, is not exactly our favorite kid to sit for. We like almost all of our sitting charges — a lot — but when Mrs. P. calls, most of us moan and groan. That's because Jenny is a spoiled brat. "Saturday?" I repeated. "From ten until three? Okay, I'll check it out and get back to you. 'Bye." I hung up.

"Mrs. P. needs a sitter on Saturday," I told my friends.

"I hope I'm busy," said Stacey, who was

sitting on the bed this time, while Dawn sat in the desk chair.

We laughed. Then Mary Anne checked the appointment pages in the record book. "You are," she told Stacey. "So are Jessi, Claud, and Kristy."

Stacey, Jessi, Claudia, and I breathed sighs of relief.

Mal, Dawn, and Mary Anne looked pained.

Then they all started saying things like, "*You* take the job, Mal. You're saving up for that set of books." Or, "You take it, Dawn. Baby-sitting for Jenny will be . . . character-building."

"Thank you," said Dawn, "but I have enough character already."

Finally Mary Anne said, "Oh, *I'll* sit for Jenny. I usually end up with the Jenny-jobs. I can handle her."

So I called Mrs. P. back to tell her Mary Anne would be sitting. Then the seven of us waited for the phone to ring again. It didn't, and finally Claud said, "Tell us more about Susan, Kristy."

I had sat for Susan twice since I'd first met her on Friday, so there was a fair amount to tell my friends.

"Autism," I began, "is so strange. It's like

56

Susan is keeping a secret from the world. Mrs. Felder describes Susan as retarded but says she *isn't* retarded, strictly speaking. I mean, she doesn't have Down's syndrome or anything. Her IQ is very low, but that's because her teachers can't test her. She won't talk. Why? She looks right through people as if they're not in front of her. She acts blind and deaf, even though she can see and hear. Why? And how can you test a person who doesn't talk and is so closed off? You can't. That's why Mrs. Felder says Susan is retarded — because she's eight, yet she acts like a two-year-old — a *slow* two-year-old. But if her teachers or doctors could reach her, who knows what she could learn."

"Anyway, what about the piano-playing and the calendar stuff?" said Jessi.

"Well, that's another thing that's so strange," I said. "Most of the time Susan acts like she's two — she doesn't dress herself very well or talk or anything — but how many two-year-olds do you know who can play classical piano?"

"None," said Mal.

"And this business with the calendar," I went on. "Today I told Susan my mom's birthday and Susan immediately said 'Sunday' and she was right! Mom was born on a Sunday. How does she do that? I mean, you can just stand there and say any date, like July thirteenth, nineteen-thirty-one, and she'll say, 'Monday' or whatever, without missing a beat. Oh, also, today I tried to trick her. I said 'February twenty-ninth, nineteen eighty-five,' and Susan said very clearly, 'March first, Friday.' You know why? Because there are twenty-nine days in February only if it's a leap year, and nineteen eighty-five wasn't a leap year. Susan knew it immediately. But she still gave me the day that fell after February twenty-*eighth*."

"Amazing," said Claudia, shaking her head.

"You know what's the worst?" I asked.

"What?" said Dawn.

"That Susan is so isolated. She's practically an outcast. Her parents send her away to school, and she doesn't have any friends, of course. I bet if her parents kept her here and put her on the school bus everyday to go to the special class at Stoneybrook Elementary, she'd fit in. She'd get to know kids in the neighborhood, maybe she'd learn how to play with them — "

I was interrupted by the phone. Several calls came in, and we lined up three jobs. The last of them was for the younger Hobart boys across the street.

Mal's face turned pink. "Oh, *please?*" she said. "*Please* could I have that job? I know we're not supposed to ask, but . . . please? Just this once?"

"Relax, Mal," said Mary Anne. "You can take it if it's okay with Stacey. You two are the only ones free that day."

Stacey grinned. "Mal can have the job."

"Oh, *thank* you," said Mallory rapturously.

After a few moments of silence (no ringing phones), Jessi said, "I was thinking, Kristy. You described Susan as an outcast. You know what? The Hobarts are sort of outcasts, too. Just because they have accents and say things like 'brecky' for 'breakfast' or 'jumpers' for 'sweaters,' or use slang words that we don't understand like 'rev heads,' the kids here are *so mean* to them. They torment them. It's as if they're prejudiced against them."

"Yesterday," spoke up Mal, "Jessi and I took my sisters and brothers over to play, though, and the kids had a fine time to-gether."

"Mal and Ben had an especially fine time," added Jessi mischievously.

Mal turned the color of a tomato.

Stacey started to say something, but I interrupted her. I couldn't help it. I'd just had one of my great ideas.

"You know what?" I said slowly. "On Friday, when I baby-sit for Susan again, I'm going to take her over to the Hobarts'! Won't that be perfect? Susan needs friends, the Hobarts need friends. Susan won't tease the Hobarts, and I bet they won't tease her. Not after the teasing *they've* been through. So I'll introduce them. Maybe if Susan makes friends by the time this month is up, her parents won't send her away. Maybe they'll let her go to school here."

"*And*," added Mal excitedly, "I could bring Claire and Margo to the Hobarts' on Friday. They got along really well with the two youngest boys. Then James could play with Susan — they're the same age — and I — I — "

"You could what?" teased Stacey.

I liked Mallory's offer a lot. I really did. But I was beginning to be suspicious of it. Did she have some other reason for wanting to bring her sisters to the Hobarts' on Friday?

"Does Ben get teased as much as his younger brothers?" asked Claud thoughtfully. (Now that we knew Ben went to our school, we kept our eyes out for him, but the eighth-graders don't have much to do with the sixth-graders.)

"I don't think so," replied Jessi. "Do you, Mal?"

Mallory, her face still fiery, just shook her head.

Jessi hid a smile. "What Mal is trying to say," she translated for the rest of us, "is that Ben is tall for his age, so he looks sort of . . ."

"Menacing?" supplied Dawn.

"No! Just like someone you don't want to mess with. Plus, at Stoneybrook Middle School we're so busy changing classes and stuff that most kids just haven't bothered Ben. But at home it's different. When the kids are out in their yard, they're easy targets. And James and Mathew and especially Johnny aren't very good at defending themselves."

"I bet Mal could help Ben feel right at home here in the USA," Stacey pressed.

Mal couldn't speak. She stared at the floor. The rest of us grinned at each other. And Stacey couldn't let up on Mallory.

"Come on, Mal. Admit it," she said. "You've got a crush on Ben."

Mal gasped. And then she was saved by the

bell. My own mother called needing a sitter on an evening when I wouldn't be home. Mary Anne lined Stacey up for the job.

Then Stacey immediately said, "Mal? Come on. Out with it. You know you've got a crush on Ben."

"Well . . . well, maybe I — I do," Mal spluttered.

"He *is* cute," said Stacey.

Mallory twisted her head back and looked up at Stacey. "He's adorable," she corrected her. "He's even got cute glasses."

Everyone laughed.

Mallory got to her feet then and stood at Claudia's window. The Hobarts were outside, as usual. This time, James was on a skateboard, Mathew was riding his bike, and Ben was helping Johnny balance on another skateboard.

"Ben is an awfully good brother," said Mal. "And he's polite and funny."

"Is he thrifty, honest, clean, hard-working, and considerate of old ladies?" asked Claudia with a smile.

Mal turned away from the window, looking as if she were in the middle of a wonderful dream. "Yes," she replied.

"Then I think you should, you know, go after him," said Dawn.

"Me? Go after a *boy?*" asked Mal.

"Sure. Why not?"

"Well, okay," said Mal quickly. "I think I will."

# CHAPTER 7

O n Friday, Charlie dropped me off at Susan's as usual. I ran up her driveway and along the Felders' front walk, and rang their doorbell. I could hear piano music and knew Susan was playing away. She didn't stop, though, when the bell rang, and she was still playing when her mother opened the door. Mrs. Felder looked tired.

"Hi," I said brightly.

"Hi, Kristy," replied Mrs. Felder. "Boy, am I glad to see you. I really need a break. This has not been one of Susan's better days. She won't leave the piano without a struggle, and trying to get her to eat lunch was like — well, you'd have thought I was asking her to eat hot peppers. She never did eat anything."

"Gosh, I'm sorry," I said.

"Anyway, pry her away from the piano if you can," Mrs. Felder went on, as I stepped inside. "I'd love for Susan to get some fresh air today, but if you can't do that, don't worry about it."

"Okay," I replied uncertainly, thinking of the plans Mal and I had made involving the Hobart boys.

I must have sounded worried, because Mrs. Felder quickly assured me, "Really. There's nothing to be concerned about. Susan is just being stubborn today. I promise. She doesn't get violent. But she's strong, and she's great at passive resistance. If she doesn't want to eat, she simply clamps her mouth shut."

"Why didn't she want her lunch today?" I asked.

Mrs. Felder shrugged. "Lots of autistic children have eating and sleeping problems," she told me. "Susan is one of them."

I nodded. "All right. Well, I'll try to get Susan outdoors. And if she'll eat something, is that okay? Or would you rather she waited until dinner?"

"No, a snack would be fine. Try a cookie, anything. I want some food in her."

Mrs. Felder left then, as if she couldn't escape fast enough.

I watched Susan at the piano for awhile. She played intently, her head cocked to the side, staring into space. She never looked at the keys. And of course, no music was in front of her, since she memorized everything.

"Susan," I said after awhile.

No response. Not even a flicker of her eyes.

"Susan! *Susan* . . . SUSAN!"

The music continued. I didn't know what she was playing, because it was something classical, and what I know about classical music could fit on a mosquito's nose.

"Susan!" I called again. I walked to the piano and stood next to her. I actually waved my hand in front of her face, as if she were a sleepwalker.

Nothing.

Then ever so carefully and gently I laid my hands on Susan's. She tried to keep playing. I tightened my grip. Susan couldn't move her fingers anymore. She had to stop playing. And you know what? For a second, or maybe even just a fraction of a second, she looked at me. I mean, she looked right into my eyes with those big brown eyes of hers. Then she lost herself in her world again. Where does her mind go? I wondered.

With my hands still on Susan's, I tried to pull her away from the piano. She wouldn't budge. I pulled harder. I could see what Mrs.

Felder meant about passive resistance. But I wasn't about to give up. I've learned plenty from my younger brothers and sisters.

Since Susan was sort of small for her age, I just moved behind her, picked her up, and carried her into the kitchen. She struggled a little, but not much.

"Okay, Susan. Time for a snack. Anything you want," I said.

Still holding one of her hands, I opened the refrigerator door. "Is there anything here you'd like?"

Susan was gazing out the window, flapping her free hand. Well, at this rate, I'd never get her to the Hobarts'. I closed the refrigerator, spotted a baggie full of homemade oatmeal cookies on the counter, grabbed a couple of them, and took Susan and the cookies outdoors.

On the way to the Hobarts', I handed her a cookie.

Susan must have been starving after her day of playing and not eating, because she took the cookie and ate it hungrily. She ate the other one, too, before we were even in the Hobarts' yard.

Since getting Susan away from the piano had taken so long, Mal, Claire, and Margo were already at the Hobarts'. Everyone was in the backyard. Mal and Ben were sitting on the stoop, lost in conversation, and the younger kids were playing tag.

"Hi!" I called, as Susan and I entered the yard.

"Hi," said some of the kids tentatively. None of them had met Susan before, and she *did* look a little odd, staring above the heads of the children, clicking her tongue, and flapping her hands.

Silence followed.

Mal looked up and saw what was going on. She and Ben joined us. "Everybody," said Mal, "this is Susan. She's eight, just like you, James. She can't talk, but I think she'd like to play with us. Oh, and Ben, James, Mathew, and Johnny, this is my friend Kristy. She's the president of the Baby-sitters Club."

"Hi," I said.

"Hullo," replied the boys cheerfully.

Claire stepped over to Susan. "I'm Claire," she said. "I'm five."

*Flap, flap, flap. Click, click, click.*

"I *said*," said Claire, "I'm Claire and I'm five."

(Susan didn't answer, of course.)

"She doesn't talk," Mal reminded Claire.

"Not at all?"

"Well, a few words when she wants to," I finally answered. "But she can't have a conversation with you."

"Why not?" asked Mathew.

The kids were standing in a circle around Susan, staring at her. She was oblivious to them.

I tried to explain about autism.

Then Margo said, "Maybe she can play tag with us. You don't have to talk to play tag."

"Yeah!" exclaimed James. "Maybe we could teach her to play."

So we tried. First, we decided that James would be It. He would chase the kids slowly around the yard, just to show Susan how the game was played.

"Run, Susan, run!" I cried.

Susan wandered under a tree. She looked up to where the sun was filtering through the branches and began waving one hand in front of her eyes. Under her breath, she hummed the music she'd been playing on the piano earlier.

Then we tried to get Susan to chase the other kids. That didn't work, either, of course.

We were still shouting, "Run, Susan!" when two of the boys who'd regularly been teasing the Hobarts sauntered into the yard. One was a good six inches taller than the other.

"Hey, Crocs," said the short one.

No one answered him.

"What? Are you all deaf?" he asked.

"Funny as a funeral," muttered James.

"What was that?" asked the taller boy. He stood imperiously over James.

At that point, Ben walked up behind him and tapped him on the shoulder. The boy turned around. He didn't look so tall anymore. He probably didn't *feel* so tall anymore, either. He backed away. And then he caught sight of Susan.

"Who's that?" he asked. "And what's she doing?" (Susan was flapping and clicking and humming under the tree again.)

"Her name is Susan Felder," I spoke up. "Who are you guys?"

The boys looked at each other. "We're Bob and Craig," said the tall one. "Yeah, he's Bob and I'm Craig," agreed the short one, just as the other one said the same thing.

"Afraid to use your real names?" I asked.

"Funny as a funeral," said Bob-or-Craig, obviously mimicking James.

Why, I wondered, did the teasers continue to come back? They must have been fascinated by the Hobarts. Otherwise they wouldn't keep egging them on. Maybe they *liked* hearing new words and phrases and names for things. But the teasers were so *mean*. If they wanted to hear Johnny ask for "fairy floss," or Ben call someone a "rev head," or Mathew talk about "brecky," they could just ask the boys to tell them about Australia. Most teasers, I had found out, tease because they feel inferior and need to feel superior — like a bully who beats up the runt of the school because the runt is easy to beat. However, *I* knew this — but it didn't help the Hobarts much.

Ben and Mal and I put our heads together and had a conference. We decided to let the kids try to work things out for themselves. And so the teasers kept teasing. In the middle of the worst of it, though, I noticed something. James was eyeing Susan. When Bob-or-Craig (the short one) stood in front of her and began flapping and clicking right in her face, James ran to Susan and put his arm around her protectively.

"Leave her alone," he said. "She's — she's my mate."

Susan had a friend! My heart soared. And then I got another of my ideas. Even though Mallory and Ben and I had decided to stay out of things, I joined James, Susan, and Bob-or-Craig.

"You won't believe this," I said, "but Susan is *really smart*."

"Yeah, right," said the teaser. "Sure she is."

"No, really." I explained that Susan had a calender in her head. "Go on," I said. "Give her any date. She'll tell you the day of the week it fell on."

"Okay," said Bob-or-Craig (the tall one) with a smirk. "December first, nineteen eighty-three."

"Thursday," said Susan woodenly.

"That's right!" exclaimed the boy. "That's my sister's birthday. How did she know that — and so fast?"

"Oh, that was probably easy for her," I said. "Go back further in time. Do you know the birthdate of one of your grandparents or something?"

"I do," said the shorter boy.

Susan performed her trick again.

Everyone was aghast — the teasers, the Hobarts, the Pikes.

I felt extremely proud of Susan.

# CHAPTER 8

Friday

Kristy, there is never a dull moment at your house, that's for sure. I baby-sat for David Michael, Emily Michelle, Karen, and Andrew while Watson and your mom went out to dinner, Nannie went out with her friends, your brothers went to a party, and you had a special job with Susan.

Karen wanted to play "Let's All Come In" and convinced the rest of us to play. The game was pretty funny, especially since Emily had no idea what was going on. She was just pleased to be a part of things.

By the way, I've been thinking about what you and I discussed when you came home, but I don't have any answers yet...

Stacey arrived at my house at a hectic time. Nannie was rushing out the door, afraid she'd be late meeting her friends. Sam and Charlie were standing in the kitchen, begging. They'd remembered that they'd promised to bring food — potato chips or something — to the party they were going to, and not only had they forgotten to pick anything up, but they were broke.

"Gee, you wouldn't be broke if you had a great job like mine," I said.

Boy. If looks could kill. Sam and Charlie gave me Dagger Eyes.

I shrugged. Then I led Stacey into the den. On our way I could hear Mom saying to my brothers, "You mean neither of you has *any* money?"

In the den were Karen, Andrew, Emily, and David Michael. They were watching *The Wizard of Oz* on the VCR.

"Remember," I said, "you can only watch until Dorothy leaves Munchkinland. Then the TV goes off."

"You're not in charge," replied David Michael, never taking his eyes off the set. "You don't make the rules tonight."

Mom appeared in the doorway. "You can

only watch until Dorothy leaves Munchkinland," she said. "Then the TV goes off."

"Darn," said David Michael.

"Bullfrogs," said Karen.

Sam and Charlie left then, each carrying a bag of potato chips, which Watson had probably given them. And then I left with Mom and Watson. They were going to drop me off at Susan's, and the Felders were going to bring me back later.

Stacey was alone with my little brothers and sisters. She sat on the floor and watched the movie with them. "Okay," she said after awhile. "Dorothy's outta there. Time to turn the set off."

Some minor arguing followed.

"She's not out yet," said Karen. "She's on the Yellow Brick Road and she hasn't met the Scarecrow. So I think she's still in — "

The Scarecrow appeared on the screen at that very moment.

"Okay," said Stacey. "Dorothy is now *definitely* out of Munchkinland." She switched off the TV.

"Aw, what are we going to do *now*?" complained David Michael.

"Play checkers?" suggested Andrew halfheartedly.

"*I* know!" exclaimed Karen. "We can play 'Let's All Come In.' We have to teach Emily the game."

"Let's All Come In" is a game my little brothers and sisters play. Karen invented it, though, and she likes it better than any of the others. She usually has to coerce the others to play with her. That's because Karen takes all the best parts for herself and gives the other parts to everyone else. See, the game is supposed to take place in a hotel lobby. One person (usually me) has to be the clerk at the desk. Another person (usually David Michael) has to be the bellman (bellperson?), who takes people's luggage to their rooms. Karen gets to play all the guests, or to assign guest roles to Andrew and Emily. She always makes them play the roles like babies or pet dogs or something.

Anyway, since everyone dresses up and changes costumes frequently for "Let's All Come In," no one minds the game much. In fact, I think they like it, but they just won't admit it.

"Costumes, everybody!" cried Karen as soon as Stacey and the others had agreed to play.

They trooped upstairs to the playroom,

where the most incredible box of dress-up clothes sits. Honestly. When I first met Watson and his kids, I couldn't *believe* the stuff in this playroom — and Andrew and Karen only visited their father two weekends a month. David Michael and Emily didn't even live in this house yet.

As you can imagine, in the trunk are costumes like you'd expect to see only in the fanciest toy store. So David Michael suited up in a pretty impressive bellman's uniform, and then Karen directed the others in their costuming.

"Now," she began, "I will be playing Mrs. Kennelworth, a very, very rich lady who is going to stay at the hotel. Emily, you will be my little girl. Andrew, you will be my pet monkey."

*"What?"* cried Andrew.

Karen ignored him. "David Michael, you go downstairs and get ready in the living room. Stacey, you go with him and make sure you have a pad of paper for our guest book."

"Okay," agreed Stacey. She and David Michael went into the living room and waited for the others to arrive.

A few minutes later, "Mrs. Kennelworth" made her entrance. She was *very* dressed up.

Karen had found a long, fancy-looking dress, silver high heels, a sequined hat, a fake-fur muff, and plenty of necklaces and bracelets.

"Good evening," said Karen. "I am Mrs. Kennelworth, here for the night with my — " (she turned around and pulled Emily and Andrew into the living room) " — with my little girl, Perdita, and my little monkey, Spunky."

In came Emily wearing her Sunday best — a white dress with pink ribbons down the front and her black Mary Jane shoes — and Andrew wearing a hat with ears on it, mittens for paws, and a realistic-looking tail.

"I'm sorry," said Stacey, the desk clerk. "No monkeys allowed in the hotel. Only people."

"But my dog — my *Mexican shorthair* — came last time," replied Karen. "Besides, I am very, very rich, and anyway, where are my lovely little girl and I going to stay tonight if we can't sleep here? We're on our way to Istanbul, you know. . . . Bellman, take our bags. Here's a one hundred-dollar tip."

Stacey pretended to look agitated. "Very well then, Mrs. Smellyworth — I mean, Mrs. Kennelworth. Sign the register, please. Sign in Perdita and Funky, too."

"Spunky," Karen corrected her. She turned

to Emily. "Say, 'Thank you, nice lady,'" she instructed her.

Emily *loves* being included in the game. "Fank oo, nice wady," she repeated proudly. (She has no idea what she's saying when she repeats these things.)

"Say, 'My, but what a beautiful hotel,'" Karen went on.

"My booful tell," said Emily.

The game continued. Karen registered at the hotel as a witch with her ghost and black cat, as an old lady with her grandchildren, and as several more characters. She was dressing for the part of a professional tennis player on tour when I returned.

"The Felders came home early," I explained, as Andrew and Emily threw themselves at me, hugging my legs.

"Oh," said Stacey. "Well, my mom can't pick me up for another hour. I'm stuck here. I hope you don't mind."

"Not at all," I replied.

Stacey and I sat on the couch in the living room.

"David Michael," I said, "why don't you be the desk clerk for awhile so Stacey and I can talk."

"Goody," replied my brother. "This uniform is *hot*."

"How was Susan?" Stacey asked as soon as we sat down.

I shrugged. "The usual. You know what makes me mad? I told her mother about James saying Susan was his friend, but Mrs. Felder didn't seem to care. She's still sending Susan away to that new school. I wish she could let Susan try living at home. That's where kids belong, I think. You know, I plan to show Mrs. Felder just how 'normal' Susan can be. I want her to change her mind about the school."

"I know you do," answered Stacey. "Just don't go overboard."

"I won't," I sighed. "You know, even I have to admit that Susan is one of the most handicapped kids I've ever seen. She wouldn't let me touch her tonight. I couldn't get her pajamas on her, and she kept screaming."

Stacey sighed, too.

And at that moment Emily, wearing a huge hat, long gloves, and high heels, came over to us and said, "Scooze me. I have dance?" (Karen was standing behind her, grinning.)

"Of course you may," I replied.

And I forgot about Susan as the grand hotel became a grand ballroom.

## CHAPTER 9

"Susan . . . *Susan* . . . Susan?"

Guess where I was. At the Felders' again, of course. Susan's mother had just left for the afternoon, and Susan was lost in her world of piano music.

For the life of me, I could not attract her attention.

I thought of putting my hands over hers, as I had done before, and stopping the music, but her mother had said she'd had a good day so far. She'd eaten breakfast and lunch, she'd behaved herself on a walk, and she had only just begun playing the piano.

Besides, for the first time since I'd started sitting for Susan I noticed a look of absolute rapture on her face as she played. She was still staring off into space, her head cocked, but she was smiling beautifully and she looked relaxed. (Usually she's wound up tighter than a tick, as Watson would say.) So I let Susan play.

I was sitting in the living room with her, about to begin my homework, when the doorbell rang.

Maybe, I thought excitedly, it was James Hobart, coming to play with his new "mate."

I dashed to the Felders' front door, peeked out the window, and saw a boy there. He was not James. In fact, he was one of the kids who'd been teasing the Hobarts. He was the short Bob-or-Craig.

I opened the door, frowning, "Yes?" I said. Maybe he had a paper route and the Felders owed him money or something.

"Hi," said the boy nervously. "Can I come in? I'm here to see Susan."

"You are?" I could hardly believe it. Still, it was great! Another friend! "Come on in," I told him.

"Thanks." The boy stepped inside. "Where is she?"

I pointed to the piano.

"You mean she plays the piano, too?" he asked incredulously.

"Yup. She can play almost anything. Do you have a favorite song? She — she takes requests," I added grandly, as if Susan were performing at a party or a wedding.

The boy stepped over to the piano. "Play 'Way Down Upon the Swanee River,' " he said, clearly expecting Susan not to know the song.

Susan switched flawlessly from whatever she'd been playing to "Swanee River." She played and played.

"Doesn't she ever stop?" asked the boy.

"I don't know," I replied. I hadn't heard Susan play anything but classical music up until now (her mother said it was her favorite) and all classical music seems long to me.

"Okay," said the boy. "Okay. Hey, Susan, play 'Monster Mash.' "

*"Monster Mash"?* That was a silly old rock-and-roll song. Susan would never kn —

But she did know it. She switched from "Swanee River" to "Monster Mash" without missing a beat.

"Wow," said the boy, awed.

"Listen, what's your name?" I asked the boy. "I mean, what is it *really*? Are you Bob or are you Craig? If you're going to be Susan's friend I should know, so I can tell her your name, and talk to her about you."

"Oh," said the boy, shifting uncomfortably from one foot to the other. "Well . . . well, the truth is I'm Mel Tucker."

"Mel," I repeated, smiling. "I'm Kristy Thomas, Susan's baby-sitter."

Mel just nodded. Then a grin lit up his face as he regarded Susan at the piano again. "I know!" he exclaimed. "I just saw *The Music Man*. That was a good movie. We rented it and I watched it three times before we had to return it. Hey, Susan, play that song about Marian, the librarian."

Again, Susan began the new song, only this time Mel's eyes nearly fell out of their sockets when Susan began to sing, too. She knew every word of the entire song. When she finished it, she began again. I had a funny feeling Susan knew every song from the movie.

"She has a pretty voice," said Mel, which was probably the highest compliment he could muster.

"She does, doesn't she?" I replied, and wondered why Susan couldn't use that voice to talk with people instead of just to sing songs she'd memorized and to give dates.

"I guess," Mel went on, "that Susan knows lots and lots of songs."

"Just about any one you can think of," I bragged.

"And I guess she can sing to all of them?" This was a question, not a statement.

"No," I replied. "Not all. But when she does know a song, she knows the whole thing. She's even memorized some songs in other languages."

"You mean she can speak Spanish and Italian and stuff?"

"Not really. It's just that if she hears a song sung in a different language, then that's how she memorizes it."

"She just *memorizes* things?" asked Mel. "How fast?"

"First try, sometimes. I mean, she hears a piece, she can play it. She hears a song, she can sing it. Sometimes it does take more than one try, though," I admitted. "That's what her mother said."

"Gosh, Susan is amazing. I was at a circus once and I saw a chicken that could play this little piano with its beak. I thought *that* was amazing. But this is even better. Susan is *really* amazing."

I smiled. "Yeah. She's special."

"She should go on one of those TV shows

about incredible people," Mel continued. "Really. She should."

"I don't know . . ."

"Well, I have to go now," said Mel abruptly. Then he added, "How often do you baby-sit for Susan?"

"Three times a week," I replied. "Mondays, Wednesdays, and Fridays after school."

"Okay. Well, I better be going. See you around!"

Mel let himself out the front door.

"Susan!" I squealed, running to the piano. I sat next to her on the bench. "You have *two* friends now! Do you understand? Two *friends*. Two people who like you. Well, make that three friends, since I like you, too. Your friends are named James, Mel, and Kristy. I'm Kristy. *I'm* Kristy. Me," I added, pointing exaggeratedly to my chest.

"Susan, you can stop playing that song about the librarian now," I said, changing the subject. "You've played it practically forever. Let's go outside."

Susan continued playing.

The doorbell rang again.

I answered it. This time James Hobart was on the front steps.

"Hi, James!" I cried.

"Hullo. Can Susan come out and play?" he asked.

Talk about music. Those words were music to my ears. "Sure she can," I answered. "But come on inside for a few minutes first."

James followed me into the Felders' house. Immediately, he said what Mel had said just a little while earlier: "You mean she plays the piano, too?"

"Yup. But it's time for her to stop," I said, thinking that if I heard Susan sing, *"I love you madly, madly, Madame Librarian, Marian,"* again I would scream. "Sometimes stopping her is a little difficult," I informed James.

I placed my hands over Susan's and tightened them until she couldn't play freely anymore.

"I — I don't want her to stop playing if she doesn't want to," said James.

"Don't worry. I don't think she *does* want to, but it's more important for her to make friends."

"That's true," said James as I coaxed Susan into her sweater. "I know exactly how Susan feels."

"I thought you might."

I took Susan by the hand, and without being asked, James took her other hand. We led her into the backyard and sat under a tree.

"In Australia," said James, "I have lots of friends. I have two pen friends, too."

"Pen friends?" I repeated.

"Oh, um, here in America you call them pen pals. Now they're the only friends I have left, and I've never even met them. One lives in England and the other lives in Canada. Oh, well. At least we can write letters."

"A real friend would be better, though, right?" I said.

"Right," agreed James. "Someone I can ride bikes with and go skateboarding with. Someone who could show me around Stoneybrook. Someone who could teach me what American kids say."

James looked so lonely that I put my arm around him. Then he put his arm around Susan, who didn't pull away. But something was wrong, I thought. I couldn't put my finger on it, but something was wrong.

The three of us sat under the tree for nearly an hour, James and I talking, Susan clicking her tongue and staring at something no one else could see.

# CHAPTER 10

"Attention, please! Attention, please! There will be an assembly in the auditorium immediately following homeroom. Everyone is expected to attend. Thank you."

I sighed. I had just gotten to school. It was early in the morning, I was tired, school assemblies are usually boring, and my locker smelled. The only funny thing was that our public-address system wasn't working too well, so the announcement sounded like this: "A-ention, ease. A-ention, ease. . . . will be an . . . embly in the au-i-orium mediately foling ome-oom. Every-nn is ex-ted to a-end. -nk oo."

Luckily, the PA system had been working like this for quite awhile, so I understood the announcement perfectly.

"*Darn,*" said Mary Anne, running down the hall and leaning dramatically against the locker next to mine. "What do you think *this* assembly will be about? The dress code? The food fight the seventh-graders had last week? Or . . . *dum da dum-dum* . . . student government?"

"Good morning, Mary Anne," I replied.

Mary Anne grinned. "Good morning. Sorry about that. It's just that assemblies — especially ones about student government — are — "

"Boring? Dull? A brain-numbing waste of valuable time?"

*"That's* it!" cried Mary Anne. "A brain-numbing waste of valuable time." She began to laugh.

"I agree," I said. Then, "Ew. . . . I wonder what this used to be." I pulled a plastic baggie out of the back of my locker. Something in the bag was very mushy and very moldy.

"Oh, dis*gu*sting!" exclaimed Mary Anne, who is easy to gross out.

"So that's what smelled so bad," I said. "I thought it was my gym suit."

Mary Anne looked like she might barf if I went on, but she was rescued by the first bell for homeroom, which rang then. She darted away, calling over her shoulder, "See you in the brain-numbing assembly!"

"Okay," I called back.

* * *

Thank goodness we don't have to sit with our classes during assemblies. The members of the BSC like to sit together, and we hardly have any other chances to do that at school because of Mal and Jessi. They're in an entirely different grade, so we don't even get to eat lunch together.

There's just one group at SMS that stays together always — in assemblies, at lunchtime, anytime. They don't even change rooms during the day. That's the class for handicapped students. A bunch of the kids in the class are retarded, and the others have different kinds of problems. Guess where the BSC sat during the assembly? Right behind the special class. The kids in that class took up exactly one row, plus three kids who sat in the aisles in wheelchairs.

Mary Anne had been wrong about the assembly. It wasn't about our dress code, the food fight, *or* student government. As a surprise, to celebrate something going on at school called Kids' Week, our principal had organized a program for us. For once, it was fun. First a really famous author talked to us about the books she writes. She had traveled all the way from Arizona just to come to SMS.

That made me feel sort of important. Then a songwriter sang a song he had composed about our school. Finally an artist called five teachers onto the stage and drew funny caricatures of them.

Did I pay attention to any of this? Barely. And why wasn't I paying attention? Not because the program was brain-numbing. For once, it was fascinating — but I couldn't pay attention because I was so busy watching the kids in the class in front of me.

At one end of the row were two of the kids in wheelchairs. (Their chairs were placed one in front of the other so as not to block the aisle and be a fire hazard.) The kid sitting in the front chair couldn't even hold herself up straight. She was strapped in everywhere — her arms strapped to the armrests, her feet to the footrests. Her head was even strapped to the back of the chair. And somehow, she managed to slump anyway. I'd seen her around school before. She tries to talk sometimes but she's harder to understand than our PA system. Her eyes don't focus on anything. She looks like she doesn't have a bone or a muscle in her body. Somebody once told me she has cerebral palsy.

The boy in back of her didn't need to be

strapped in so much. He could sit up, but he was mostly paralyzed (I think). He couldn't even talk. Once I'd passed his class and looked in. I'd found out how he communicates. He holds a special stick in his mouth and uses it to tap out messages on a computer keyboard. Guess what. He can make pictures by holding a paintbrush or a pencil in his mouth. Claudia says his pictures are good, and she should know.

The first three kids in the row next to the ones in the wheelchairs were all retarded. They have Down's syndrome. I read about that in a book. Down's syndrome people have sort of slanted eyes and flattish faces, and are usually docile, affectionate, and friendly.

Next to them was a boy who was so hyperactive that on his other side sat a teacher's aid whose only job was to keep him still and quiet during the program. I'll tell you something. That kid was paying a lot more attention to the program than I was. That was what he was excited about. He kept pointing to the stage, or trying to jump up, or turning to the teacher and saying, "Oh, *neat!* Oh, *neat!*"

The girl on the other side of the teacher was deaf and blind. The boy next to her was deaf. (How, I wondered, did the teachers teach so many different kinds of kids all in one class-room? The deaf boy probably wasn't retarded. The blind and deaf girl probably wasn't either, but I bet she learned a lot differently than the deaf boy did, and both of them must have been much more advanced than the retarded kids.)

Anyway, it was the kid in the second to the last seat in the row — next to a teacher who was between him and the third kid in a wheel-chair — who really attracted my attention. Guess why. Because the boy reminded me so much of Susan. Every now and then he would clap his hands together for no apparent rea-son. (Nobody else was clapping when he was.) A couple of times he waved his right hand back and forth in front of his eyes. But what was most interesting to me was that some-times he would stare off into space — and *talk*. Mostly, he spoke quietly, so I couldn't hear him, but a few times he spoke more loudly. Once he said, "How old are you?" and another time he said, "Stop it, Jerry." They were meaningless sentences (or else just out of con-text), but at least he was *talking*. That was impressive enough, but my jaw dropped wide open when he turned to his teacher and said, "Go home, please? Go home?"

"No, Drew," replied the teacher patiently. "Not yet. Later."

"No, *now*," said Drew. "Go home *now*."

Drew could carry on a conversation! It was wonderful. I was certain he was autistic. But if Drew could talk, I thought, so could Susan. Furthermore, Drew did not attend some fancy away-from-home school. He had made more strides than Susan had, and he had probably made them right here in the Stoneybrook public schools. So why, why, *why*, did the Felders have to send Susan away? Why couldn't they do what Drew's family had done? Keep Susan at home — and let her learn in a familiar environment. Drew seemed to be way ahead of Susan. Maybe that was because he'd been kept at home.

I was still thinking about Drew and Susan, when Mary Anne elbowed me in the side.

"What?" I whispered. She was probably going to tell me to pay attention — which would irritate me. She is not a teacher.

"Kristy," she said. "Look." She pointed discreetly across the aisle.

There I saw two sixth-grade boys laughing hysterically at a third boy who had crossed his eyes and was letting his head roll around.

I couldn't believe it. They were making fun

of the girl in the wheelchair. Why didn't someone stop them?

Then a girl next to them wadded up a little piece of notebook paper, rolled it around in her mouth, and threw the spitball across the aisle. It hit the hyperactive boy on the side of his face. It surprised him, and right then and there, he threw a tantrum. The teacher's aid had to take him out of the auditorium.

Luckily, another teacher had seen what the sixth-graders were up to, and *they* were taken out of the auditorium, too — to the principal's office, I hoped.

I felt so angry I wanted to scream at those kids. I wanted to shout, "Haven't *you* ever been teased? Hasn't anyone ever thrown a spitball at *you?* I hope someday someone finds out something you're sensitive about and blabs it to the whole school. I hope they publish it in the newspaper!"

I was also upset. I had just seen a drawback to going to a handicapped class in a "regular" school. The "normal" kids could tease or laugh at the handicapped ones. That wouldn't happend to Susan if her parents sent her away to school. But I still thought she should stay at home.

When the assembly was over I gathered up

my courage, told my friends I'd see them later, and stepped up to the teacher of the handicapped kids.

"Excuse me," I said. "I know you're busy, but I was wondering a couple of things about your class."

I thought the teacher might be aggravated with me for interrupting her when she had so much to do, but she looked pleased that I was interested.

I relaxed. "That boy," I whispered, trying to point without his seeing me. "Is he autistic?"

"Yes," replied the teacher, looking surprised. "How did you know?"

I told her a little about Susan. Then I asked a couple of questions about how she and the aid ran their classroom.

"Would you like to visit our room sometime?" she offered. "Maybe during a study hall? You'd be welcome."

"Well . . . sure," I replied. "I *would* like that."

At the end of school that day, during the mad rush of opening and closing lockers, Mary Anne and Dawn caught up with me just as I was closing my own locker.

"Hey, look!" cried Dawn.

Mary Anne and I turned in the direction Dawn was looking. There were Mallory and Ben walking through the hall together, their hands touching lightly.

"Notice anything?" said Dawn.

"Yeah," I replied. "I think Mal's in love."

"Not that," said Dawn. "What I mean is — no one's paying a bit of attention to Ben."

"*Oh*," I replied. Hmm. Either the older kids didn't care that Ben was Australian — or the Hobarts were beginning to be accepted.

# CHAPTER 11

" 'Bye, Mrs. Felder. Have fun!" I called, as Susan's mother left through the garage door.

To be perfectly honest, Mrs. Felder looked as if she were escaping. She was on her way to the beauty parlor to have her hair col — I mean, cut (that was exactly what Mrs. Felder had said!), and to get a manicure and a pedicure. She said that an afternoon at the beauty parlor was just what she needed to relax. And she *did* look as if she needed some relaxation. Some rest, too. She said Susan had barely slept the past three nights — and that when Susan was up, Mr. and Mrs. Felder were up as well. Susan screamed and cried and whined when she was up at night. No one knew why. She also prowled the house. Mrs. Felder said she and her husband had considered locking Susan into her room at night, but that they just couldn't bring themselves to do it.

I was glad.

I closed the door after Mrs. Felder and turned around to face Susan. I had planned to take her over to the Hobarts' to see James that afternoon, and I wanted to catch her before she could sit down at the piano.

Just as I was taking her hand, the doorbell rang.

"Hey, Susan! That was the *doorbell*," I said emphatically. I was hoping to help Susan pick up some vocabulary. "Let's *answer* it," I went on. "Maybe a *friend* is at the *door*. A friend for *Susan*. Maybe it will be *James* or *Mel*."

*Click, click, click* went Susan's tongue. I don't think she'd heard me at all.

I led Susan to the front door.

"Okay, Susan. *Open* the *door*," I said. I helped her to turn the knob and pull the door open. She did this with one hand, flapping the other hand in front of her eyes.

On the steps stood the tall teaser. The tall Bob-or-Craig — whose name I was now certain was neither Bob nor Craig, since the short teaser's name was Mel.

"Hi," I said, half-heartedly. (I'd really been hoping for James.) "Before you say a word, please tell me your real name."

"It's Zach," he said. "Zach Wolfson."

"Okay. Thank you. I'm Kristy Thomas, Susan's baby-sitter."

"I know," replied Zach. "I, um, I came to see Susan."

"You did?" Susan certainly was lucky. I was amazed at the number of children who were willing to play with her.

"Yeah," replied Zach. "I did. Do you think — do you think she could do the calendar trick for me again? That was great."

"Well, sure. Come on in."

I held the door open for Zach, and he stepped inside the Felders' house, staring at Susan.

"Let's sit on the floor," I suggested. "That'll be the most comfortable."

I settled Susan and Zach on the floor. No, that's not true. Zach settled himself on the floor, and I *tried* to settle Susan, but she kept squirming around and trying to stand up.

That is, until Zach pulled a rumpled piece of paper out of the pocket of his jeans and said, "August twenty-sixth, nineteen forty-three."

Immediately, Susan settled down. "Thursday," she said to the ceiling. She focused on the task, but not on Zach.

Zach consulted his paper. "Yup!" he said.

101

"Okay, June tenth, nineteen sixty-two."

"Sunday," said Susan in her monotone voice.

Zach shook his head in amazement. "Right again. Um, October twenty-fifth, nineteen fifty-four."

"Monday," said Susan.

"Yup," replied Zach after a glance at his paper. "Well, I guess I better be going. I've, um, got a lot of homework."

"Oh," I said, feeling disappointed.

Zach stood up. I started to stand up, too, in order to see him to the door. "Hey, that's okay. I can let myself out," he told me.

And he did. But he'd only been gone for a few seconds when the bell rang again.

"That must be *Zach*," I said to Susan. "He probably *forgot* something. Did you ever *forget* anything?"

*Click, click, click.*

Susan and I answered the door for the second time. But we didn't find Zach on the stoop. Instead we found a girl. I knew she lived in the neighborhood somewhere, but I couldn't remember her name.

"Hi," she said cheerfully. "I'm Kathie. Can I come in and see Susan?"

"Well . . . sure," I replied, thinking, *I* should be so popular. I turned to Susan. "You've got another *visitor*," I told her.

Kathie smiled at Susan.

Susan looked like she was heading for the piano, so I sat the three of us on the floor again. Guess what. Kathie gave Susan a bunch of dates, just like Zach had done. Then she left. She said she thought she heard her mother calling.

Why wasn't I surprised when the bell rang for a third time? I didn't even bother leading Susan to the door and talking to her about answering it or anything. I just left her in the living room and ran to the door myself. Before I'd opened it all the way, Susan was at the piano. She began playing a song from *The Music Man*. (I knew the whole score by then.)

This time another girl was on the stoop. She was holding a record album, and she introduced herself as Gina and said she'd come to see Susan. How interesting that three kids came by all in one day. Maybe *this* would change the Felders' minds about school.

Before I could say a word to Gina, she walked right inside and said, "She *can* play the piano! She really can!"

"Susan is playing a song from *The Music Man*," I told her.

"Oh," Gina replied. "Well, I was wondering if — I mean, Mel said Susan can memorize a new song if she hears it just once. Is that true?"

"Usually."

"Okay. I've got a song here — on a real old record of my grandparents — that I bet Susan doesn't know. Can she do her memorizing trick for me?"

"I guess so. Let's make sure she doesn't already know the music, though. What is it?"

" 'Sheik of Araby.' It's a Roaring Twenties song."

Whatever the Roaring Twenties are.

"Susan," I said loudly. "Susan! Play 'Sheik of Araby.' "

Susan continued playing "Wells Fargo Wagon" from *The Music Man*.

"I don't think she knows 'Sheik of Araby,' " I told Gina.

"Goody. Let's play it and see if she can memorize it."

"All right," I replied, even though Mrs. Felder had never said whether it was okay to touch the stereo. I took the record from

Gina, put it on the turntable, and practically shouted, "Listen, Susan! Here's 'Sheik of Araby.' It's a new song."

As soon as the music came on, Susan stopped playing. She sat quietly at the piano, her head cocked, as if she were concentrating very hard. In the middle of the song, the old record began to skip. It skipped six times before I could rescue it. A few moments later the song ended.

"Okay, Susan, play 'Sheik of Araby,' " said Gina bossily.

Hesitantly, Susan began to play — and then to sing. The first part of the recording had been only music, with a lot of different instruments. Not only did Susan translate the piece to music for the piano, but she came in right on cue with the words.

"How does she do that?" asked Gina.

I'd asked myself the question about a million times, but I hadn't found any answers.

Susan played on until near the end of the song when suddenly Gina and I heard her sing, "All the stars that shine above with light, will light, will light, will light, will light, will light, will light our way to love . . ."

Susan had played and sung the skips as

if they were part of the actual song. So she really *did* just memorize what she heard. The music and the words didn't have any meaning for her. I felt achingly sad all of a sudden.

But not Gina. Gina began to laugh. "She played the skips!" she hooted. "I don't believe it. She played the skips! Boy, this was really worth it."

"Worth what?" I asked suspiciously.

Gina looked alarmed.

"Worth *what?*" I repeated, as Susan began "Sheik of Araby" again.

"Nothing." Gina scrambled for her record, then dashed to the front door.

I followed her outside — and around the corner of the house, where we ran into Mel and a whole bunch of kids. Mel was holding a fistful of dollar bills.

"All right. Just what is going on here?" I demanded.

The kids grew silent.

Except for Mel. "What happened?" he asked Gina.

"*She,*" said Gina angrily, pointing at *me*, "got mad. I want my dollar back."

"Your dollar back!" I said with a gasp.

"Yeah! Mel's charging us a buck apiece to

go inside and see the incredible retard who can memorize dates and music. The amazing dumbo who can sing but not talk," said Gina.

My jaw dropped.

Mel Tucker had a real sideshow going. He thought he'd found an even better attraction than the stupid chicken he'd once seen playing a piano.

"You," I said, advancing on Mel — and I can look pretty menacing, even though I'm short. (Several children ran away.) "Do you know what you're doing? You're *using* Susan. You're making a spectacle of her." I turned to the rest of the kids. "And I don't ever want to hear any of you use the words 'retard' or 'dumbo' again. Do you hear me?"

"Yes," murmured the few children who hadn't already run off. "And as for that money, Mel, half of it — at *least* half of it, belongs to Susan. She did all the hard work. So fork over," I ordered him.

But of course he didn't. Mel and the remaining kids ran down the street. When they were about half a block away, they began to laugh. How can people be so insensitive?

And how could I have been so naive? How could I have thought those kids suddenly wanted to be Susan's friend? I should have seen through them. At least Susan couldn't see through them. I was glad she didn't know what was going on.

I needed to cool off.

So I led Susan over to the Hobarts', where I knew Claud was baby-sitting.

# CHAPTER 12

winsday

This afternoon I sat for James Mathew
and Johnny Hobart their father was at
work their mother had an apertiment
downtown and geuss where Ben was. Ben
was at the library studing whith Mallory!
The Hobart boys are good kids even wehn
other kids give them trubble. Their
finaly starting to stand up for
themselves. Like today James had to
prove himself but he ended up whith
a new freeind. Kristy you know all
this all ready becuase you came over
whith Susan right after James had
shown waht he can do.

While I was dealing with Mel Tucker and the other neighborhood kids, Claudia was sitting for the three younger Hobart boys. No wonder James hadn't come over to play with Susan. He'd been busy trying to prove that he was neither a Croc nor a wimp. . . .

Claudia's afternoon started with Johnny's tears. As soon as Johnny realized that his mother was going to leave him with someone he barely knew, he began to cry.

"Don't go!" he wailed.

"Johnny," said Mrs. Hobart gently, as Claudia stood in the front hall of Mary Anne's old house, trying to look as nonthreatening as possible, "your brothers are going to be here with you. Mathew and James are here."

Johnny stood on tiptoe and tugged at his mother's shirt. Mrs. Hobart bent down so Johnny could whisper to her. She listened for a moment. Then she smiled and said, "No. I promise that Claudia will not call you a Croc."

"I promise, too," said Claudia. "I'll only call you Johnny."

"What do I call you?" Johnny asked Claudia, holding his mother's hand.

"You can call me Claudia or Claud — or whatever you want. Gabbie Perkins next door sometimes calls me Claudee Kishi. She likes to call people by their first and last names."

Mrs. Hobart smiled at Claudia, and Claudia smiled back. She thought how similar the Hobarts looked, with their reddish-blond hair, their round faces, and the smattering of freckles across their noses. Even Mrs. Hobart had freckles. Claudia hadn't seen Mr. Hobart close up, though, so she didn't know whether he had freckles.

"All right, Johnny, I have to leave now," said Mrs. Hobart.

"No!" squawked Johnny.

"Mathew! James!" called Mrs. Hobart. "Can you please come here?"

The boys clattered down the stairs.

"I'm leaving now," their mother told them. "Please give Claudia some help with Johnny. Oh, and Johnny, you can help Claudia, too. I don't think she knows where the telly is. Or maybe you'd like to offer her a lolly."

"Lollies? We can have lollies?" asked Johnny.

"Yes. If you'll let go of my hand."

Johnny let go. He made a dash for the kitchen, and Claudia said good-bye to Mrs. Hobart. "Everything will be fine," she assured her. "Don't worry."

The Hobart boys and Claudia each helped themselves to a lolly. (No way was Claudia going to turn down an offer of junk food.) Then Mathew said, "Let's watch the telly. I like Big Bird and Oscar the Grouch."

"Me, too," agreed Claudia, "but do you really want to stay inside on such a nice day?"

"I do," spoke up Johnny, who was already a sticky mess.

"He doesn't want to be called a Croc," said Mathew.

"Do the kids *still* call you Crocs?" asked Claudia.

"Yes, but not as much," admitted James.

"Then let's go out to your backyard," said Claudia. "Johnny, you can bring your new truck out. We'll have fun. Honest." She gave Johnny's hands and face a wipe with a wet cloth.

"*We're* going out," said James, speaking for himself and Mathew.

"Then I'll come, too," Johnny said finally.

So Claudia and the Hobarts ventured outside, Johnny clutching his truck.

The boys played peacefully for twenty minutes. Johnny steered the truck around the yard, making sound effects as he went. James and Mathew played on a swing that their father had made for them. It was a huge tire suspended from a tree branch by a thick rope. The boys could stand on the tire and swing back and forth together.

"Awesome!" yelled James as he and Mathew swung higher and higher.

"Slow down!" was Claudia's horrified reply. Ever since she was little she had heard that it was possible to swing so high you went right over the top of the swing set or the tree branch, making a complete circle. She had never known if that was true, but she didn't want to find out while she was baby-sitting and have to explain to the Hobarts that their sons had done a three-sixty on the tire.

"Yeah, slow down," echoed a voice.

Claudia turned around.

Johnny brought his truck to a stop.

And James and Mathew jumped off the swing.

Zach Wolfson had entered the Hobarts' yard. Claudia didn't know it, but he had come straight from the Felders' house, where he had paid Mel a dollar to ask Susan the three dates. (I realized later that Zach had not been among the kids hanging around Mel when I had charged out of Susan's house after Gina.)

"Pay attention to your baby-sitter . . . you *babies*," teased Zach.

"We are not babies," replied James hotly.

"Yes you are."

"No we're not."

"Yes you are."

"Well, *I'm* not," said James. "I'm even in advanced maths in my new school."

"Advanced maths? *Maths?* You can't even say the word right."

"What word?"

"Math. It's *math*, not *maths*. . . . James, can you say *math?*"

James didn't miss a beat. "Zach, can you say *How would you like your head bashed in?*"

"Sure," replied Zach. "How would you like your head bashed in?"

James had fallen into his own trap.

He turned and marched out of the backyard. When he came back, he was carrying an old wooden crate and a boxing glove. He set the box on the ground near Zach.

"Watch this," said James. He put the glove on and smashed his fist clear through the top of the crate, almost to the ground.

Claudia knew better than to ask James if he was okay. She knew that he and Zach had to have this out (whatever it was) between themselves and on their own terms.

Zach's eyes widened. "Whoa," he said. "What was that? Crocodile Dundee stuff?"

"No," replied James.

"Karate?" asked Zach.

"No. I'm just strong. Very strong. Think how you'd look if that crate had been your face."

Zach winced. Then he backed away. He looked a little frightened.

But James said, "I could teach you to do that."

"You could?"

"Sure. All you need are big muscles. Do you have big muscles?"

"Well . . . well, maybe I would if I worked out. . . ."

James nodded knowingly. Zach was a bully, but probably not a bad kid.

"You want to go bike-riding sometime?" Zach asked James.

"Yeah! That would be ra — that would be great. Or how about skateboarding? Do you have a skateboard?"

"Of course."

"We could go skateboarding now," said James. "You could borrow my brother Ben's if you don't want to go home for yours. He'd let you. He's awfully nice about things like that."

It was at this point that I stormed into the Hobarts' backyard with Susan in tow. I fully expected James to run to Susan — his mate. Instead he waved, but turned back to Zach.

"Hello, everyone!" I called.

"Hi," replied Claudia and the boys.

"Here's Susan," I announced needlessly.

"Hullo, Susan," called James.

"Claud," I said, "I have to talk to you." Then I added, "James, can you play with Susan while I talk to Claud?"

"Can — can Susan skateboard?" asked James doubtfully.

"I don't think so," I replied.

"Oh. Zach and I were going to go skateboarding." James looked quite pleased to be able to say "Zach and I" as if Zach were a celebrity. He also looked hesitant. I could tell he didn't want to hurt Susan or disappoint me.

"Hey, that's okay," I said. "You guys go on. Susan will be fine with Claudia and me."

Johnny went back to his truck, Mathew went back to the swing, and Claud and I sat on the stoop. Susan stood nearby. She refused to sit down for some reason.

"So you know what that Mel Tucker was doing?" I said indignantly as I finished telling Claud about the afternoon's events.

Claudia leaned forward. "What?"

"He was charging the kids around here a dollar to go into the Felders' house and either ask Susan dates or get her to memorize a new piece of music. It was like she was a freak or something. Mel was calling her 'the retard who can memorize dates and music' and 'the dumbo who can sing but not talk.' "

"That's — that's terrible!" cried Claud. Then she lowered her voice. "Are you sure you should say that in front of Susan?"

I looked over at Susan, who was standing exactly where I had left her. As usual, her hands were flapping away. She was staring at the sky, weaving her head from side to side.

"You know, I really don't think she hears us. I don't think she knows who we are. I don't think she even knows where she is. Worse, I don't think any of that matters to her."

Claud's eyes filled with tears. So did mine.

"Where does she fit in?" I asked.

"Maybe not here," replied Claud sadly.

117

"Maybe not with 'regular' kids."

Susan and I spent the rest of the afternoon at the Hobarts'. James and Zach played the time away. Zach never asked Susan to join him, but he called "hullo" to her every now and then.

James had found the kind of friend he needed. The friend was Zach.

# CHAPTER 13

There have been very few jobs in the history of the Baby-sitters Club that I *really* did not want to go on, and today's job was one of them. Oh, sure, there have been times when I didn't look forward to sitting for Jenny Prezzioso, or when I wondered what I'd be getting into when I signed up to sit for Jackie Rodowsky, the walking disaster.

But today was different.

Today was my last day at the Felders', and Susan's mother needed me not so much to baby-sit as to help pack Susan's trunk for her new school. This was a bigger job than it sounded. You might think that all Mrs. Felder would have to do was fold up Susan's clothes, put them in the trunk, and throw in a stuffed animal or two. It wouldn't be like packing for Karen, my stepsister, who would want to

119

bring along books, games, toys, her roller skates, and a lot of other things.

But it was a big job. The school had sent the Felders a list (a long one) of the belongings a new student was to bring, and each item had to be labeled with Susan's name. Plus, Mrs. Felder insisted on washing and ironing everything first. I guess she wanted to make a good impression.

The washing and ironing and labeling were not what I disliked, however. What I disliked was that we had to pack Susan's trunk at all.

I had failed in my mission to keep Susan at home, where I thought she belonged. But I did not mention this to Mrs. Felder.

Anyway, I arrived at Susan's house at three-thirty, and Mrs. Felder greeted me with a smile and an armload of freshly washed and ironed clothes.

"Hi," she said. "Come on inside."

In the background I could hear Susan singing, *"I love you madly, madly, Madame Librarian, Marian,"* and accompanying herself on the piano. Mrs. Felder and I left her alone. As long as we could hear the piano, we knew she was safe.

We carried the pile of clothes to Susan's

bedroom, where a steamer trunk was open on the floor.

"Okay," said Mrs. Felder. "There's the checklist from the school." She pointed to a piece of paper lying on Susan's bed. "The items I've checked off have been washed, ironed, folded, labeled, and packed. I don't check anything off until all five things have been done. That way, I know I'll send Susan off in good — " Mrs. Felder paused, and her eyes looked awfully bright. I could tell she was trying not to cry, and I hoped she wouldn't. (I never know what to do when an adult cries, especially an adult I don't know very well.) "Off in good shape," Mrs. Felder finished, apparently getting control of herself.

I guessed that sending Susan away again wasn't easy for Mrs. Felder. There were times when I thought that packing her off was the Felders' idea of the easy way out. But Susan *was* their only child. It couldn't be easy to let her go.

"Can you sew?" Mrs. Felder asked me.

"A little," I replied. (I hate sewing, but I can do it if I have to.)

"Good. These clean clothes in the basket need Susan's name tags sewn inside them.

The job goes faster than you'd think."

"Okay," I replied, as Mrs. Felder handed me a threaded needle and then threaded one for herself.

We settled into our work. At first we didn't talk. The sounds of "Gary, Indiana," another song from *The Music Man*, floated upstairs.

"Today Susan is playing the score from the movie," Mrs. Felder informed me. "She's playing the songs in the order in which they're played on our record."

I nodded. Then, from out of the blue, I asked, "What was Susan like when she was little?" I think I asked because I was looking around her room and it reminded me of a hotel room — no personality. No indication of what kind of person the room belonged to. There were no posters on the walls, no books, and very few toys, because Susan didn't care about such things.

That was sad. Even my littlest sister, Emily Michelle, who is only two and barely talking, has much more of a personality than Susan. We *know* her. Emily already has strong likes and dislikes. As soon as she came to stay with us she developed a fascination with teddy bears. So there are bears all over her room, and pictures of teddies on her walls. She likes balloons, too, so we got her a lamp that's shaped like a bear holding a bunch of balloons, and someone made her a mobile of bears and balloons, and Nannie is knitting a sweater for her with bears and balloons on it.

There are no secrets with Emily. Not like Susan, who is all locked up and so secretive we don't know her.

"When Susan was little?" Mrs. Felder repeated. "You mean when she was a baby? Or when she was a toddler?"

"Both, I guess," I replied. I knotted a thread, cut it off, folded one of Susan's shirts, name tag in place, placed the shirt in the trunk, and put a mark on the checklist.

"Well," Mrs. Felder began, looking faraway, "I know this sounds silly — I guess every mother says it, or at least thinks it about her own child — but when Susan was born, my husband and I agreed that she was the most beautiful baby we'd ever seen. We thought she was perfect. She wasn't all scrunchy and red-faced and bald like the other babies in the nursery." (I smiled.) "She was born with curly dark hair, and she had wide eyes with long lashes and her face was just, well, perfect."

"She *is* beautiful," I broke in.

"Thank you," said Mrs. Felder. Then she

went on, "Her father and I counted her fingers and toes and exclaimed over her tiny, tiny nails — just like all the other new parents were doing with their babies.

"Anyway, we brought Susan home and she was so *alert*. Our pediatrician assured us she was very advanced. She did everything early. Held her head up early, sat early, crawled early, walked early, talked early. She was speaking in sentences before we knew it. She even taught herself to read. Mr. Felder and I thought we had a genius on our hands. We looked into progressive schools for Susan and dreamed of the great future we were sure she'd have. We put money away so she could go to the best possible college someday. . . . We never imagined we'd be spending that money on the school she's going to now." (I felt a lump rise on my throat and hoped *I* wouldn't cry.) "But then," said Mrs. Felder, "when Susan was two and a half, she just — just shut down. She stopped speaking, stopped playing, even started wetting her pants, and she'd been toilet-trained for over six months. The pediatrician said it was the 'terrible twos,' but it soon became clear that that wasn't the problem at all. This was when I taught her to play the piano. It was the only way I could reach her. And it was a way to be near her, since she wouldn't let anyone touch her or hold her anymore. Apart from the piano, she became fascinated with the oddest things, like little pieces of paper that she'd wave in front of her eyes. When she found her father's perpetual calendar we *let* her be fascinated with that because it seemed more . . . normal. It seemed *smart*, not like hand-flapping or paper-twirling. But soon it became an obsession, like the piano. That was how she learned the years and dates.

"By the time Susan was three and a half, we'd lost her completely. She's pretty much now the way she was then, except that she's toilet-trained again, for the most part, and can dress herself and feed herself, with a lot of prompting."

Wow. I hadn't expected to hear all of that. I was trying to think of what to say to Mrs. Felder when the piano-playing stopped.

"I'll go check on her," I said.

I ran downstairs to find Susan wandering through the living room.

"Mrs. Felder?" I called. "Susan looks sort of antsy. Do you want me to take her outside?"

"That would be great," replied her mother. "She's been indoors all day."

So I led Susan out the Felders' front door, although that was clearly not something she wanted to do. She pulled at my hand and made a strange, whining noise.

But I was determined. "We're going for a walk," I told Susan resolutely. "Maybe we'll see your friend James."

It took a lot of pulling, but I managed to walk Susan around the corner to the Hobarts'. There we found James and Zach, Johnny — and Jamie Newton! So Johnny had made a friend, too.

"Hi!" I called.

"Hullo!" replied James, ever cheerful. "Hullo, Susan!"

Susan had picked up a leaf. She was twirling it in front of her face.

"That girl," Zach began, eyeing Susan, "is the weirdest — "

He was stopped by a look from James.

And Susan chose that moment to wet her pants. Right there on the sidewalk in front of everyone.

I guess I should have taken her to the bathroom before we left the house.

"We have to go home," I said lamely.

I led Susan back around the corner, feeling ashamed. I felt ashamed for both of us —

ashamed for Susan because she didn't know enough to feel ashamed for herself, and ashamed for me because . . . because . . . I wasn't sure why.

My feelings were all mixed up.

# CHAPTER 14

It was a Friday afternoon.

It was also Susan Felder's last day at home.

My sitting job was over. Nevertheless, Charlie dropped me off at the Felders' after school as usual. The Felders were leaving at four or four-thirty and I planned to be there to see Susan off.

When I rang the Felders' bell, Mr. Felder answered the door. It was the first time I'd met him. He'd been out of town the two times I'd sat for Susan in the evening. I don't know why, but I'd been expecting a serious, morose little man. What I found was a big bear of a man with a beard, a ready grin, and lots of curly hair, who greeted me with a hug.

"You must be Kristy," he said. "My wife has told me all about you. I hope you know how much you've meant to us — Susan, too — this past month."

"Thank you," I said, taken aback. (How could silent Susan have been the daughter of this easygoing, effusive man?)

"Susan!" called Mr. Felder. "Look who's here!"

He held the door open for me, and I entered the Felders' house.

Susan didn't appear, of course. She never comes the first time you call her. So Mr. Felder ushered me into the living room, where Susan was sitting tensely on the couch, flapping and clicking. She looked as if she knew something unusual was going to happen.

"Susan? Honey?" said Mr. Felder. He sat next to Susan and took one of her hands in his, but she yanked it back. "Look who's here, honey," Mr. Felder went on, undaunted. "It's Kristy. She came over just to say good-bye to you."

*Flap. Click.* Susan stared at something off to the left of me. She stared so intently that I turned around to see if Mrs. Felder had entered the room. But nothing was behind me except an armchair.

Susan wasn't staring. She was lost. Her mind was . . . where?

"Mrs. Felder is upstairs," Susan's father told me. "Last-minute stuff. It's hard to — I mean, we keeping thinking of things the people at the new school should know. About Susan. So Mrs. Felder began a letter and it's getting longer and longer."

I smiled. "I think I understand what you mean. You should have seen my mom when my brother and stepsister and I went to camp for the first time. She actually wrote a note to Karen's counselor saying that Karen doesn't like turnips. As if Karen wouldn't say that herself. She's such a chatterbo — "

I stopped abruptly, realizing what I'd almost said.

"Don't worry," Mr. Felder replied. "It's hard for a parent to send any child away."

"I know." I remembered what Mrs. Felder had said while we'd been packing Susan's trunk.

And suddenly, even though I'd only known Susan's father for a few moments, I felt that I could talk to him. "When I first came here," I told him, "when I first met Susan, I hoped I could change her. I hoped I could make a difference this month so that she wouldn't have to go away to school. I really thought Susan would be better off at home. I thought she could go to the class for handicapped kids at the elementary school."

"Oh, we looked into that," Mr. Felder assured me, as I sat down in the armchair, "but we felt the program wasn't individualized enough for Susan, and the teachers felt that Susan functioned at too low a level for the program. That was when Susan was five. And at about the same time, we found the school she's been attending for the last three years. Believe me, it wasn't easy sending her away at that age — it was like sending a *baby* away, and she was our only child — but we knew we had to do it.

"Now," he continued, "she's back again . . . and about to be sent away again." Mr. Felder looked at his daughter and for just a second, his twinkly eyes became the saddest eyes I'd ever seen. "But we've looked and looked," he said. "We've researched schools from here to California, and we really think the one we've found will do wonders for Susan. We're lucky it's so close by. We especially like the music program. Music is the only way we've been able to reach Susan. And if the special training can improve her music technique, too, well, who knows? Maybe one day we'll have a prima donna pianist on our hands: Susan Felder, IN CONCERT! Wouldn't that be something?"

"It sure would," I agreed, and for the first time, I began to see just how much hope parents pin on their children. I wondered what Mom had pinned on my brothers and Emily and me. Would she be disappointed if I became one thing and she'd secretly been hoping for something else all my life? Was she proud of me? Did my father — wherever he was — even *have* any hopes for me?

Then I thought of the Felders, the hopes they'd had for Susan when she was an advanced baby, and even the thin thread of a hope that Mr. Felder still clung to: Susan Felder, IN CONCERT! I was beginning to feel dangerously sad when Mr. Felder spoke up.

"I don't suppose Mrs. Felder has told you our good news," he said.

Their good news? Had they found out something about Susan's prognosis?

"No," I replied. "She hasn't."

Mr. Felder grinned. "Susan is going to become a big sister. Mrs. Felder and I are expecting a baby."

"You are?" I shouted. I couldn't help it — I jumped up. "Oh, that's fantastic! It's *wonderful*! Susan, Susan, you're going to have a baby brother or sister!" I tried to give her a hug.

"She's going to have a sister," said Mr. Felder. "We're having lots of tests done. We know we can't detect autism before the baby is born, but a lot of other problems can be detected (so can the sex of the baby), and Mrs. Felder and I aren't taking any chances. Besides, we're getting older by the minute." (I grinned.) "Anyway, so far, so good. The baby seems perfectly healthy. Her name," he added, "will be Hope."

"Oh, I just *know* Hope will be wonderful," I said. "I can feel it. She'll go to Stoneybrook Elementary. Hey, she can be friends with Laura Perkins — the baby who lives in my old house. They'll be just about the same age. And maybe one day you'll let me sit for Hopie. That's what I'll call her. Hopie."

"Hi, Kristy!" called a voice that sounded forcefully cheerful, if you know what I mean. Like the person would be cheerful if it killed her.

It was Mrs. Felder. She was heading downstairs, a fat envelope in her hand and Susan's pillow under one arm.

"Hi!" I cried. "Congratulations! I just heard your news. About Hope. I'm so excited. That's great!"

Mrs. Felder smiled a genuinely cheerful

133

smile. "Thank you," she said, patting her stomach. "Do I look any fatter to you?"

I peered at her. I never notice when people gain or lose weight, unless it's, like, a hundred pounds. "You know, I think you do," I said, because that was the answer she wanted to hear. "Yup. Just a little."

Mrs. Felder's smile became a grin.

Then Mr. Felder looked at his watch. "We better get going," he said. "The school wants us there by dinnertime. The way they introduce students to school life is to thrust them right into it. Susan's room became ready for her this afternoon, and she's expected to eat supper in the dining room with the other students at six-thirty tonight."

I nodded. "Is there anything I can do to help?"

"Could you give me a hand with the trunk?" asked Mr. Felder. "It's heavy. I don't want my wife trying to lift it."

So I helped Mr. Felder load Susan's trunk into the back of the car. Then Mrs. Felder led Susan outside. She was just about to settle her in the backseat with her pillow when we heard, "Hullo!"

Who else but James?

The Felders and I turned to see James Hobart running across the lawn toward the car.

"I came to say good-bye!" he called. "Susan's leaving, isn't she?"

"Yeah," I replied. Then I added, "Mr. Felder, have you met James Hobart? He and his family moved into Mary Anne Spier's old house."

James and Mr. Felder shook hands. Then the Felders and I kind of stood back while James approached Susan. "So long," he said. "I'm glad you were my mate."

No response from Susan.

"Susan?" said James. "Susan?"

Nothing.

James extended his hand as if he were going to take Susan's, then thought better of it, and pulled his away. "Well, good-bye," he said. "I'll miss you. I hope you come back soon."

Mrs. Felder started to cry, and James looked at me as if he might cry, too, so I put my arm around him. Then the Felders buckled Susan into the car, climbed into the front seat, and rolled down their windows.

"Good-bye!" they called as they backed into the street. "Thank you, Kristy! 'Bye, James!"

" 'Bye!" we called back.

"I wish Susan would say 'good-bye,'" said James, as we watched the car disappear down the street.

"Me, too," I replied. "Maybe she'll be able to after she's been at the school for awhile. Who knows what she'll learn there."

"Yeah, who knows," echoed James, sounding as if he didn't believe she'd learn a thing. Then he added, "My mum says it isn't nice to pity people, but I do feel sorry for the Felders. I can't help it. Susan is their only kid and she won't talk or anything. I know how that feels, because for awhile she was my only friend, and I wanted a friend who could *talk*. I wanted that really badly."

"Don't feel too sorry," I told James. "You've got Zach now, and guess what. I don't think this is a secret or anything so I'll just go ahead and tell you: Mrs. Felder is expecting another baby."

James' eyes lit up. "She *is?!* That is rad — I mean great. It's *great!*"

"I think so, too," I said.

I hung around the Hobarts' house until five o'clock, almost time for our Friday BSC meeting.

# CHAPTER 15

I went to Claudia's early. I knew she wasn't baby-sitting that afternoon, and it's nice to have a chance to spend time with my old friends. Before Mary Anne and I moved, I could pop next door to visit her, or pop across the street to visit Claudia any time I wanted. So I took advantage of being back in the neighborhood without a sitting job and went to Claudia's house early.

When I reached the top of the Kishis' stairs, I could see Claudia at the end of the hallway, bent over her doorknob.

"What are you doing?" I asked her.

"Trying to pick the lock," she replied. "You're here early."

"I know. I wanted to visit. But Claud, your door's *open*," I pointed out. "I thought you only needed to pick a lock if you were locked out — or needed to break into something."

Claudia held up a bobby pin and grinned at me. "I just want to find out if it really is possible to pick a lock with one of these."

"Why?" I asked as I slithered by her and entered the room.

"Because," she said, "you never know when you might need this skill. Besides, I want to pretend I'm Nancy Drew, cracking an important case."

"Does it work?" I asked. "I mean, does the bobby pin work?"

"No, darn it." Claudia flung the bobby pin to the floor in frustration. Then she picked it up, smiled, and said, "Oh, well. If this won't work, something else probably will. I'll just have to think creatively — like Nancy Drew." Claudia put the bobby pin in a dresser drawer, then exclaimed, "Oh, *here* they are!"

"What?" I asked.

"My Mentos. I've been looking for them everywhere. I could have sworn I put them in that secret drawer in my jewelry box." Claudia opened up the package and offered me the top Mento on the roll, which I thought was very generous of her. "Mento?" she said.

"Certainly," I replied. "Thank you." I settled into the director's chair.

Claudia took a Mento for herself, then said

suddenly, "Didn't Susan leave today? Didn't she go off to her new school?"

I nodded. "Yeah."

"I'm sorry," said Claud. "I know you wanted her to stay here."

"Well, it's funny. I *did* want her to stay, but now I think the new school is the best place for her."

"Really?"

"It took me a long time to realize it," I said, "but Susan needs help she can't get here. She's *very* handicapped. She needs more than her parents can give her, more than I can give her, more than the teachers in the public schools can give her."

"More than the *special* teachers?" Claud wanted to know.

"Yes."

"But what about those kids we sat behind during that assembly?"

"They're all more advanced than Susan."

"Even the autistic boy you told me about?"

"Yes."

"Even the *retarded* kids?"

"Especially the retarded kids. They can learn. They want to learn. They *talk*. They just go at a slower pace than the rest of us. And they're not all locked up inside themselves.

"I thought," I went on, "that if I could just introduce Susan to what a 'normal' life is — you know, living at home, playing in the neighborhood, making friends with other kids, learning games — that she would change. But she didn't. She couldn't. She needs extra-extra-extra-extra-special help."

I got up and looked out Claud's window. There were James and Zach, whizzing down the street on their skateboards.

"The Hobarts ended up fitting in," I said to Claud. "Susan didn't."

"What do you mean?" Claudia was busy changing her cactus earrings for her spider earrings.

"I mean, let's see. . . . Okay, the Hobarts moved here about the same time Susan came home from school. At first, they were all outcasts, like Jessi said. The kids around here didn't accept any of them because they were different. But it turned out that the Hobarts weren't so different after all. They stood up for themselves and fit in. But Susan was too different. Unless she changes a lot, she'll never fit in here . . . with 'regular' kids. You were the one who pointed that out to me."

I looked at Claud's digital clock, the BSC official timepiece. It read 5:20. "The others should start arriving soon," I said, and at that moment we heard someone absolutely thunder up the stairs.

"You guys! You guys!" called Mallory's voice. She barreled into the room and stood in the middle of it, her hands on her hips. "Oh, I'm glad someone's here," she said. "I would have been pretty embarrassed if I'd done all that yelling and no one was here yet."

"Well, we're here," said Claud. "What's up? Mento?" She held out the roll.

"What's up? Boy, everything," replied Mal, taking a Mento and settling herself on the floor. (Jessi and Mal *always* sit on the floor, even when they get here early and there's plenty of space available on the bed.) "First of all," began Mal, "Jamie Newton invited Johnny Hobart over to his house to play."

"Great!" said Claud and I.

"Second, Zach invited James to his birthday party. James is beside himself. It's his first American party and he can't decide what to give Zach, but he's really, really excited."

"Fantastic," I said.

"Fantabulous," said Claud.

"Third, the kids in Mathew's first-grade class voted that he should have the lead in a play they're putting on."

"Wow," said Claud and I. That really was impressive.

"How do you know all this?" I asked. "I was just over at the Hobarts' and they didn't say anything to me."

"I guess they're a little shy sometimes. Ben told me all the news. And speaking of Ben, I haven't told you the best news yet. But maybe I'll wait until everyone else gets here."

"Boy, it really must be good news," I said.

"The best. It's the *pièce de résistance*."

Claud looked blank.

I said, "The piece of resistance?"

"*No!*" cried Mal, grinning. "That's French for 'the best part.'"

"Oh," said Claud and I.

The next club member to arrive was Stacey. No thundering up the stairs for her, though. She trudged up, made her way down the hall, and flopped on the bed.

"I get the bed this time," she said wearily. "Dawn will have to sit at the desk. I'm exhausted."

"You look horrible," I said. I couldn't help it. Things like that just fall out of my mouth sometimes.

"Kristy!" exclaimed Claudia.

"No, it's okay," said Stacey. "Since I feel

horrible I'm not surprised that I look horrible, too."

"What's wrong?" asked Claud. "If you have the flu or something you should probably go home."

"I don't think it's the flu," Stacey replied. "I'm just tired. Maybe I've been doing too much lately. Going back and forth between here and New York and stuff. I've lost some weight, too. But I don't have a fever or anything."

"Speaking of losing weight," I said, "guess who's gaining weight?"

"Who?" asked the others, looking puzzled.

"Mrs. Felder. She's pregnant. They're going to have a baby, a girl. Her name will be Hope."

"Oh, *awesome!*" cried Claud, and we all began talking at once.

I hardly noticed when Jessi, Mary Anne, and Dawn arrived, but I did notice when the clock turned to five-thirty.

"Order!" I said loudly. "This meeting of the BSC will now come to order." (My friends quieted down.) "Any club business?" I asked.

No one said anything, although Mallory looked like she was going to burst from her *pièce de résistance.*

"Well, Mal and I have some news about our

clients that I feel we should share with you. I'll go first and be quick. Then Mal can tell you her news. My news is that the Felders are going to have another baby." I ran through the details again for Jessi, Dawn, and Mary Anne, who had missed out on the earlier announcement.

Then Mal told her news about Johnny, Mathew, and James Hobart. And *then* she said, "Now for the *pièce de résistance* — "

The phone rang.

"Darn, darn, *darn!*" cried Mallory, jumping to her feet. "I don't believe it! This can't be happening!"

Stacey hid her smile as she answered the phone. We arranged for a sitter for Jenny Prezzioso.

"It *would* be Jenny who would spoil my story," muttered Mal. "All right  The big news is Ben's news, too. . . . He asked me to go to the movies with him!"

Well, of course the members of the BSC began screaming, and congratulating Mallory. Most of us did, anyway. Jessi hung back, and I knew just what she was thinking. What would happen to her friendship with Mal if Mal had a boyfriend? I knew she was wondering that because I wondered the same thing when Mary Anne first started going out with Logan. I also knew that — soon — Jessi would see that she and Mal were still best friends, and that a best friend is very different from a boyfriend. The two don't usually cancel each other out.

I sat back and watched my friends congratulate Mal, and talk about the Hobarts. I let my mind wander, which rarely happens during a meeting, since I try to remain official. But it did wander — to Susan. And then to the kids in the handicapped class at SMS. Right then and there I decided something important. I decided that when I grew up, maybe I would be a teacher and work with kids like Susan.

Hey, Susan, I thought, I hope you like your school. I hope someday you'll come home and be able to tell James and me, and your mom and dad, and Hopie all about it.

Dear Reader,

*Kristy and the Secret of Susan* is based partly on my experiences as a therapist with autistic children during the summers I was in college. While there was no real Susan Felder, I met lots of kids like Susan and lots of families facing the same challenges Susan's parents face in the book. Autistic kids are very special, and I will always remember the kids I worked with. In fact, *Kristy and the Secret of Susan* is not the only book I've written centering around an autistic child. Before the Baby-sitters Club began I wrote *Inside Out*, told from the point of view of an older brother whose younger brother has autism. If you're interested in learning more about kids like Susan, check your library for *Inside Out*, or ask a librarian to suggest other titles.

Happy reading,

Ann M. Martin

L. GODWIN

## Ann M. Martin

# About the Author

ANN MATTHEWS MARTIN was born on August 12, 1955. She grew up in Princeton, NJ, with her parents and her younger sister, Jane.

Although Ann used to be a teacher and then an editor of children's books, she's now a full-time writer. She gets the ideas for her books from many different places. Some are based on personal experiences. Others are based on childhood memories and feelings. Many are written about contemporary problems or events.

All of Ann's characters, even the members of the Baby-sitters Club, are made up. (So is Stoneybrook.) But many of her characters are based on real people. Sometimes Ann names her characters after people she knows, other times she chooses names she likes.

In addition to the Baby-sitters Club books, Ann Martin has written many other books for children. Her favorite is *Ten Kids, No Pets* because she loves big families and she loves animals. Her favorite Baby-sitters Club book is *Kristy's Big Day*. (By the way, Kristy is her favorite baby-sitter!)

Ann M. Martin now lives in New York with her cats, Gussie and Woody. Her hobbies are reading, sewing, and needlework — especially making clothes for children.

# Notebook Pages

This Baby-sitters Club book belongs to _____ .

I am _____ years old and in the _____

grade.

The name of my school is _____ .

I got this BSC book from _____ .

I started reading it on _____ and

finished reading it on _____ .

The place where I read most of this book is _____ .

My favorite part was when _____ .

If I could change anything in the story, it might be the part when

_____ .

My favorite character in the Baby-sitters Club is _____ .

The BSC member I am most like is _____ .

because _____ .

If I could write a Baby-sitters Club book it would be about ____

_____ .

# #32 Kristy and the Secret of Susan

Susan Felder, who is autistic, has many special talents. She is an expert piano player, and she can name calendar dates for years to come. One special talent I have is _____ _____. Two special talents I would want to have are _____ _____ and _____ _____. The most talented person I know is _____. This person can _____ _____. Susan Felder can play any song on the piano after she's heard it once. If I could play any instrument, I would play the _____ _____. Some of the songs I would like to play are.

_____

_____ .

# KRISTY'S

Playing softball with some of my favorite sitting charges.

A gab-f

Me, age 3. Already on the go.

# SCRAPBOOK

My family keeps growing!

th Mary Anne!

David Michael, me, and
Louie — the best dog ever.

Illustrations by Angelo Tillery

Read all the books
about **Kristy**
in the Baby-sitters Club series
by Ann M. Martin